# MURDER in PASSY

*Murder in the Marais*
*Murder in Belleville*
*Murder in the Sentier*
*Murder in the Bastille*
*Murder in Clichy*
*Murder in Montmartre*
*Murder on the Ile Saint-Louis*
*Murder in the Rue de Paradis*
*Murder in the Latin Quarter*
*Murder in the Palais Royal*

# MURDER in PASSY

Cara Black

Published by
Soho Press, Inc.
853 Broadway
New York, NY 10003

Library of Congress Cataloging-in-Publication Data

Black, Cara
Murder in Passy / Cara Black.
p. cm.
ISBN 978-1-56947-882-0
1. Leduc, Aimee (Fictitious character)—Fiction. 2. Women private
investigators—France—Paris—Fiction. 3. 16e Arrondissement (Paris,
France)—Fiction. 4. Paris (France)—Fiction. I. Title.
PS3552.L297M7985 2011
813'.54—dc22
2010034816

10 9 8 7 6 5 4 3 2 1

In memory of Madame Aufrère,
Anne-Françoise's great aunt who loved Passy,
and for the ghosts.

# ACKNOWLEDGMENTS

My deep thanks to: forensic pathologist Terri Haddix, M.D., Vincent O'Neill, Jean Satzer, Dot Edwards, Barbara, Jan Gurley, M.D., Max, Susanna von Leuwen, Elaine, Libby Fisher Hellman, Jo and Don Metz, and the amazing Ailen, Katie, Mark, Bronwen, and Justin at Soho.

In Paris: Colonel Michael McGurk, American Embassy, Paris, André Rakoto, Service Historique Ministère de la Défense, Chateau de Vincennes, Sarah Schwartz, translator extraordinaire, Gilles Fouquet, Carla Bach, toujours Anne-Françoise Delbègue, Gilles Thomas, underground specialist, Julian Pepinster, of the Paris Métro, the GIGN unit at Satory, Versailles for the visit and expertise, Vassili, gracious Silvie Briet of Eau de Paris, Nathalie and Benoît Pastisson, generous beyond words.

*Un grand merci* in Passy and Auteuil to Anne Bordier, Lynn Green-Rutannen for our walks over the years, Arianne Rosenau Levery for sharing her "village," and Claude Pasquét.

On the Basque front, La Maison Basque de Paris, Jean Damien Lesay, and in Bilbao, Elizabete Bizkarralegorra, huge thanks, and Ondo Izan.

Always in my corner, James N. Frey, Linda Allen, my son Tate, and Jun.

Words feel inadequate for the debt I owe my late, dear editor Laura Hruska. Her guidance and knowledge over the years were a gift. *Merci*, Laura.

"What is irritating about love is that it is a crime that requires an accomplice."

—CHARLES BAUDELAIRE

# PARIS
November 1997

*Monday Early Evening*

THE DOORBELLS TINKLED as Aimée Leduc stepped inside the cheese shop from the cold and inhaled the warm, pungent odors. A radio blared the evening news: ". . . evading seven roadblocks erected after the shootout in the *Imprimerie Nationale* documents heist. In other breaking news, a radical faction. . . ." She shivered, nodding to pink-faced, rotund Victor, standing in his white apron behind the counter. Bombings, shoot-outs, she hated to think what else—and to make it worse, just before the holidays.

"World's gone crazy." Victor shook his head. "The usual?" He gestured to a runny rind on grape leaves standing on the marble-topped counter: "Or this?"

Aimée tasted the Brie dripping on the white waxed paper. "*C'est parfait.*"

She emerged from the shop into the evening mist and rounded the corner toward her office on rue du Louvre. The reflections of the furred yellow orbs of streetlights glowed on the wet pavement.

"About time, Leduc." Morbier, her godfather and a police commissaire, his black wool coat beaded with moisture, paced before her building door. An unmarked Peugeot with a driver, engine thrumming, waited at the curb.

"More like five minutes early, Morbier." The chill autumn wind cut a swathe through the street of nineteenth-century buildings. Passersby hurried along, bundled in overcoats.

A look she couldn't read crossed his face. "We've got a situation in Lyon. I'm late. You've got the file, Leduc?"

Forget the apéritif she'd expected in the corner café! She brushed away her disappointment. So they would do the exchange in the cold, wet street. She handed Morbier a manila envelope containing the supposed ten-year-old letters and photo of her "brother" Julian. It was time to let the professionals handle the only copies she had, so she could find out once and for all if they were genuine. "A week for lab authentication, Morbier?"

In return, he showed her an engraved business card reading POLICE PAPER FORENSICS DIVISION HEAD PAUL BERT. "Bert's the leading forgery expert. That's all I know."

She nodded; she couldn't push it. He was doing her a favor.

"Time for a quick espresso?" She pointed to the lit windows under the café's awning, which was now whipping in the wind.

Morbier shook his head. Under the thick salt-and-pepper hair, his face appeared more lined in the streetlight; dark circles showed under his eyes. "You think life finally makes sense, then . . . *alors*," he shrugged. "*Pouff*, it turns upside down."

"What's wrong, Morbier?" She wished they were inside the warm café with its fogged-up window instead of standing in the wind. A siren whined in the distance. "A case?"

"Can't talk about it, Leduc."

As usual. The streetlight revealed his cuffed corduroys, his mismatched socks, one brown, one black. Morbier was no fashion plate. He hadn't made a move toward his car. Unlike him.

She sensed something else bothering him. His health? "Did you have that checkup like you promised?"

"Something's going on with Xavierre," he said. "I'm worried."

Taken aback, Aimée fumbled for something to say. She remembered him with his arm around Xavierre, an attractive older woman with dark hair. Xavierre's laughter, warm smile, and scent of gardenias came back to her.

"Worried over what?"

"She doesn't answer her phone," he said.

"*Zut!* I don't either, half the time," she said. "You're reading too much into it."

"I need to know what's going on."

She'd never seen him like this, like a lovelorn shaggy dog. It was not often that he shared his personal feelings.

"Her daughter's getting married soon, *non?*" Aimée rubbed her hands, wishing she'd worn gloves. "You told me yourself last week. She's busy." A cloud of diesel exhaust erupted from the Number 74 bus as it paused to board passengers.

"Xavierre's holding back," he said. "Something feels wrong, Leduc. When my gut talks, I listen."

"Like what? You're thinking she's in danger?"

"She's fond of you," Morbier said. "Help me out, eh?"

He hadn't answered her question. "But what can I do?"

He pulled a police notepad from his coat pocket and wrote down an address. "Do me a favor. Her daughter's wedding rehearsal party's tonight. Go there and talk to Xavierre. She'll open up to you. If I hadn't gotten called away to this investigation—"

"*Me?*" Aimée interrupted.

"How many times have I helped you, Leduc?" he said. "Better get going, the party's started."

Why did she always forget that Morbier's favors had a price?

He pointed to the leather catsuit under her raincoat. "I'd suggest you change into a little black dress, too."

"*You* dispensing fashion advice, Morbier?"

But he merely said, "Can I count on you?"

She nodded. And then he climbed in the waiting Peugeot. A moment later it turned and its red taillights disappeared up rue du Louvre. Some kettle of fish, she figured, if they had to summon Morbier to Lyon.

She hit the numbers on the digicode keypad; the door buzzed open. She was tired out: it had been her first day back at work after a month's recovery from the explosion that had laid her low on her last case. Her shoulders ached; she had a report to file. And now this. But she couldn't ignore the urgency in Morbier's voice.

On the third floor, she unlocked Leduc Detective's frosted glass door. Instead of the dark office she expected, she caught the sweet smell of juniper logs and welcome warmth emanating from glowing embers in the small marble fireplace. "What are you doing still here, René?"

René Friant, her partner, a dwarf, swiveled his orthopedic chair, his short fingers pausing on the laptop keyboard. "Catching up," he said. "How did today's surveillance go?"

He was worried about their computer security contracts, as usual.

"I think you'll like this." She slotted the VCR tape into the player. Hit PLAY.

René's large green eyes scanned the screen. With an absent gesture, he brushed at the crease in his charcoal suit pants, which were tailored to his four-foot height.

"Good work." René grinned.

She'd had a tête-à-tête with the VP of operations and had planted the video camera in his office, along with a data sniffer on his office computer's input cable. Now they could monitor his less-than-transparent budget transactions remotely. Their client, the CEO, needed proof of embezzlement.

"So the VP took the bait?"

"Like a big hungry fish, René." She crinkled her nose in distaste. "The things I do for computer security!"

René shrugged. "And for a fat check, too. We should be able to document the VP's sticky fingers in the corporate cookie jar and wrap up our surveillance by Friday, write our report, *et voilà*."

He was excited, as always, on a new project. She hadn't realized how much she'd missed work while spending a month on her back. She had been wounded and René hospitalized after being shot. But René had recuperated at a seaweed Thallasotherapy, a cure courtesy of national health insurance. Noticing his glowing complexion, she wished she'd done that too, instead of attempting to master the new encryption manual while she recovered.

"I need to run an errand for Morbier." She glanced at the time. "Back in an hour. Then I'll lock up."

"Leaving now? You just got here."

"*L'amour*, René."

"Eh? Another bad boy? Don't you learn—"

Was that anger in his voice? She ignored it.

"Not me. Morbier's worried about Xavierre, wants me to talk to her," she said. "It's complicated."

"You're serious?" he said. "We've got an account to update. And there's this case."

"Do you think I don't know that?" she said. The last thing she wanted was to go back out into the cold. "But Morbier called in a favor."

She took the half-empty Orangina off her desk, tore off a piece of baguette from inside her bag, unwrapped the white waxed paper, and scooped up a runny wedge of Brie. Dinner.

"Help yourself, René." She went behind the screen and unzipped the black leather catsuit, peeling the buttery leather from her thighs. She found her little black dress with the scooped neck, vintage Chanel, in the armoire and hooked the last snap under her arm. She clicked open her LeClerc compact and applied a few upstrokes of mascara.

"Armed in Chanel." René shook his head. "You look tired."

So obvious? She noticed the circles under her eyes and dabbed on concealer, ran her *rouge noir* nails—for once newly lac-quered—through her shag-cut hair. She had blond highlights this week, at her coiffeuse's suggestion. She checked the address on the map in her Paris plan. "40 rue Raynouard, that's in the 16th *arrondissement*."

"*Très chic*," René said. "Look, it's your first day back; let me give you a ride."

"But it's out of your way," she said. "I'll grab a taxi."

"Morbier's my friend too, Aimée," he said, sounding hurt.

"That's not the issue, René."

His health was. He was still using a cane. The case she'd dragged him into last month had resulted in his injuries; she didn't want that to happen again. "No reason for you to get involved."

"But I already am." He shut down his laptop. "My car's out front."

\* \* \*

TO THEIR LEFT, the arms of the Seine wrapped the Île de la Cité in a turgid gel-like embrace. Arcs of light from the gold-crowned Pont Alexandre III glittered on René's Citroën DS windshield as he shifted into third gear. The dark masses of trees lining the quai whizzed by, blurring into a row of shadows.

Concern dogged her as she recalled the tense edge in Morbier's voice, the tremble in his hand. She doubted he'd had that checkup. She pulled her anthracite-gray faux fur tighter. The heated leather seats toasted her thighs.

It was late, she was tired, and part of her wanted to get this over with. The other part wondered what Morbier's gut had told him.

"Morbier thinks she's seeing another man, n'est-ce pas?" René turned onto a wide avenue with tall limestone Haussmann buildings like silent sentinels to the quartier, which was bordered by the Seine and the Bois de Boulogne.

"I don't know," she said.

"But that's a special thing, eh," René said. "Older men offer the devotion of a lifetime, as Oscar Wilde said."

More to it than that, she thought as they drove past closed upscale boutiques. Past Franck et Fils, the darkened department store where her father had bought her Catholic school uniform, and the shuttered café opposite where they'd had hot chocolate, something she longed for on a night like this.

René turned onto a street canopied by trees. The next narrowed into a high-walled lane; no doubt it had been a cow path in the last century. It still amazed her how these enclaves existed, tucked away, the remnants of another world: the old villages of Auteuil and Passy, where once Roman vineyards had dotted the hills, thermal springs—celebrated for curative properties—had beckoned seventeenth-century Parisians, and where Balzac, penniless and in debt, had written while hiding from his creditors.

René turned the corner and pulled over, and the Citroën shuddered to a halt. She stepped out of the car into a biting wind under a sky pocked with stars. It was a cold clear night.

"Quiet, *non?*" René said.

"Deafening." Only the chirp of a nightingale could be heard as the fallen chestnut husks crackled under their feet.

Now the *quartier* housed embassies in old *hôtels particuliers* amid exclusive countryside-like hamlets of the moneyed who could afford tranquility.

Aimée pressed the intercom at the side of the high wall front-ing No. 40, which was bathed in pale streetlight.

"*Oui?*"

"Madame Xavierre?"

"You have an invitation?"

She felt uneasy and cleared her throat. "Commissaire Morbier asked me. . . ."

"*Un moment.*" Aimée shivered as dead leaves swirled around her ankles. Voices and strains of classical music drifted through the intercom. René's breaths showed like puffs of smoke in the night air.

A moment later, the grilled gate buzzed open.

They stepped into a small garden, a *jardinet*, fronting a Louis Seize–era townhouse. Trellised ivy climbed the stone façade. Twin horseshoe stone staircases ascended to the entrance of this small jewel of a mansion. Even wearing vintage Chanel, she didn't feel comfortable in this kind of place.

René whistled. "Not bad, Aimée. We win the Lotto, we can live here too."

Morbier, a dyed-in-the-wool Socialist, with a *haute bourgeoise* girlfriend? Opposites did attract. Several Mercedes were parked in the gravel driveway, which ended in a dark clump of buildings.

After buzzing the door, they entered a black and white tiled foyer. Beyond open double doors, a high-ceilinged room revealed a chandelier. The clink of glasses drifted toward them.

René unwound his Burberry scarf, putting his gloves in his coat pocket. Then he stopped. "You're paler than usual, Aimée. Sure you want to go through with this?"

She applied Chanel Red to her lips. Blotted it with a torn deposit slip from her checkbook. "Better?"

Determined, she strode inside, where she saw a blue banner hung across the gilt-paneled wall. It read BON MARIAGE, IRATI ET ROBBÉ in silver letters. Inside, the closeness of body warmth lingered. Coming from the cold into the stuffy room made her feel light-headed.

Where were the other guests?

It was only 7:30, but the cake had been cut. Smudged Champagne flutes stood on the sideboard. Only an old couple remained: a man wearing a formal black dinner jacket, a woman in a black dress more suited to a funeral. They'd seen sixty a long time ago.

René tiptoed to reach for the last of the Champagne. His fingers couldn't quite reach it. Aimée, with a deft swipe, took a flute of fizzing rose Champagne and handed it to him.

"Vintage Taittinger. Not bad." He shot Aimée a look. "But not what I'd call Morbier's crowd."

She agreed.

The old man, cadaver-thin and shrunken in his black jacket, winked at her. Already well into the Champagne, he had a happy glassy look in his eyes. "Don't tell me," he said. "You're another cousin, eh?"

"We come in four-packs, like yogurt," Aimée said as she scanned the room. "You don't just marry the daughter, you get the family."

A petite young woman, dark hair knotted in a clip, wearing a slim red skirt and a silk blouse, stepped into the room. Her large dark eyes were hesitant. The man took a look at her, grabbed his wife's hand, and left.

Odd.

"*Excusez-moi*, are you Irati?" Aimée asked. "I'm Aimée Leduc."

A blank stare greeted her. Had she made a mistake? Aimée noticed clenched white knuckles clasping the silk blouse. Then the girl gave a little nod.

"Sorry to bother you," Aimée said. "I know you're busy. But Morbier asked me to speak with Madame Xavierre."

Irati smiled. "Not at all. This gives me a good excuse to extricate *Maman* from the temperamental caterers. Now I can escape upstairs and sleep. My fiancé, Robbé, escaped already." Her voice quavered; she paused. "But I know you, don't I?"

"I'm Commissaire Morbier's goddaughter."

"Of course." A look Aimée couldn't decipher crossed her face. The tinkle and crash of plates sounded from the kitchen. Irati clenched her fists together.

"*Pardonnez-moi*, Aimée," Irati said and left the room.

René downed his Champagne. "A real love feast, eh? Temperamental caterers, a wedding party of geriatrics, a sweet girl. And we rushed out into the cold for this?"

She wondered herself. A cigarillo moldered in a crystal ashtray.

Beside it was a half-eaten slice of *gâteau* Basque oozing with cherries and almond filling.

Aimée caught a whiff of gardenia, felt her shoulders grasped, and then Xavierre's warm cheek pressed on hers in a flying kiss. "Aimée, delightful to see you."

Xavierre's peach silk scarf framed her shoulders. Matching lipstick, a hint of blush, and arched brows in an unlined face. Not one dark hair out of place. If she was surprised, she didn't show it except perhaps by a little jump in the pulse at her neck, barely discernible in the dim light.

Aimée introduced René. Xavierre shook René's hand, holding his in her own peach nail-lacquered fingers, her gaze level, not averting her eyes as do most people confronted by a dwarf. "Morbier late as usual? As you see, the guests have left."

"*Désolé*, Xavierre, I'm his messenger." She hesitated, sensing a tautness in Xavierre, an undercurrent. "Can we talk in private?"

She took Xavierre aside near the tall salon door and lowered her voice. "A last-minute investigation came up. He asked me to tell you in person."

"But why? He went to too much trouble. I'm fine."

"You didn't answer your phone." Aimée hesitated. "He worried. . . ."

"My phone?" Xavierre blinked. Then laughed. "*Zut!* I guess I forgot to charge it."

Aimée nodded. "I forget all the time too. But is anything wrong? I mean. . . ."

A line tightened at the corner of Xavierre's perfectly applied peach lipstick. "Have you ever planned a wedding on two weeks' notice?"

Aimée shook her head, feeling awkward. Did that explain it?

She couldn't ask Xavierre if she was having an affair. Not her business. But she could put in a good word for Morbier. "I've never seen Morbier so happy, Xavierre."

Xavierre smiled, squeezing Aimée's hand. Her look was wistful. "But we met more than twenty years ago. He hasn't told you? A *coup de foudre*, love at first sight." She gave a little sigh. "My marriage, his, children, divorce got in the way. But when I ran into him last month, we reignited. It was as if we'd never said good-bye."

A phone trilled from the hallway. Xavierre's eyes clouded. There was a flutter of fear in them. Her shoulders tensed, and then she seemed to relax. Aimée heard the click of heels in the hallway and then Irati answering the phone.

Xavierre sighed. "I've got so much to do for the wedding on Sunday. I'll reach Morbier later. I think it's better if you go now." Xavierre took a deep breath. "You understand, *non?*"

Aimée could understand. But not the flicker behind Xavierre's eyes and the tight smile. Family problems? Or something else?

"*Maman?*"

"You'll need to excuse me." And without another word, Xavierre left.

Aimée heard footsteps coming from the kitchen. A moment later, Irati stood at their side.

"*Maman's* upset; let me apologize for her," Irati said. "The wedding plans, stress of relatives, endless. Me, I'm calm. Supposed to be the other way round, *non?*" She gave a short laugh.

Short and forced, Aimée thought. What undercurrents are flowing here? she wondered.

"Maybe it would have been easier if Morbier had been here," Aimée said.

"Nothing would help." Irati blinked, then looked away, distracted.

What did that mean? Time to disregard tact and force the issue. "Morbier was worried she was having an affair," Aimée said.

René shot her a look.

"You're saying my mother would—" Irati said.

"Me and my mouth," Aimée interrupted. "Please forget you ever heard that, Irati." Aimée paused. "Your mother's upset. Can I help?"

"Right now I wish this were all over," Irati said.

Not exactly the excited bride-to-be, Aimée thought. "What's wrong?"

Pause. "Robbé and I wanted to keep it simple. But you didn't hear that either." Irati took Aimée's arm. "In Basque, when things go badly, we say it's like cobwebs: just brush them away and get on with it. I'll see you both out."

Outside, the crisp biting wind met them. The air cleared Aimée's head, but did not dispel her unease. Xavierre was hiding something.

"What do you make of that, René?"

"A tempest in a teapot," he said with disgust. "Morbier's over-reacting."

She wished she thought so too.

"But, considering the Taittinger," René said, smiling, "not a totally wasted trip."

Fir branches scraped the wall, their scent released into the crisp air. Beyond, at the side of the house, was the service entrance. A dim glow shone from windows, pooling yellow on the gravel.

"Give me a moment," she said, unable to get rid of her sense of unease. "I'll be right back."

She walked over the gravel toward the kitchen's back windows. For a moment she sensed a presence. A feeling that someone was watching them. As she was about to look up from the crunching gravel under her feet, she heard a squishing sound. Her shoe's pointed toe was mired in softness. Leaves, and something else, clung to her red-soled Louboutin heels. Then the smell hit her. Dog poo!

Great.

She heard the gate click open.

"*Un moment*, René."

She leaned against the stone wall, took the penlight from her bag to see to clean off her shoe, and shook her head. "My brand-new heels, too!"

In the penlight's beam, she saw by the tan smeared dog poo several reddish-brown congealing clumps on her shoe sole. She grabbed a twig to scrape it all off. There was a coppery metallic smell. She looked closer.

Blood.

Her hand froze. "René," she whispered.

"What now? I'm cold." He let the gate shut. His gaze traveled the penlight's beam, which traced a reddish-brown trail of droplets over the gravel path along the ivy-covered wall.

"I don't get it." René shook his head. "It's late. Let's go, Aimée."

From behind the house, Aimée heard a car start. The rumble of a diesel engine, the spit of gravel as it took off. She tiptoed ahead, rounded the corner, crouched under the windows. Shadows flickered. She saw movement inside the house.

"It's not our business." René stood behind her next to green garbage bins by the short flight of back steps.

"Shhh." She leaned toward him, tugged his elbow. "He thinks we left."

"Who?"

"The figure watching from the window," Aimée said, pointing at the house. "He heard the gate close."

Hunched down, she poked with the twig, noticing that the blood had darkened. It had semi-clotted in the cold night air. The blood was not fresh, but not old enough to have dried. She followed the blood spatter trail on the gravel around the corner to the garden.

Her penlight beam illuminated the evening-misted hedgerow, a tangled fragment of peach scarf, and, farther on, a figure slumped among the gooseberry bushes against the stone wall. Fear jolted along her spine.

"Xavierre?" Her throat caught. "You all right?"

But the cocked angle of Xavierre's head, the scarf twisted tight around her neck, and her unblinking gaze told Aimée that Xavierre wouldn't answer now. Couldn't.

"My god, René! Call the SAMU!"

He flipped his phone open.

Horror-stricken, Aimée untied the scarf digging into Xavierre's flesh. She felt for a pulse. None. Frantically, she made quick thrusts to Xavierre's chest.

"*Maman?*" Irati's voice came from the open French doors. "Telephone for you."

Too late.

Wind rustled the damp leaves tattooing shadows across Xavierre's pale face. "What's going on?" Irati said. "What have you done to my mother?"

"Her heart's not beating, Irati."

"I don't understand." Then a piercing scream. Irati knelt down by Xavierre's lifeless body, stroking her mother's cheek. "You killed *Maman!*"

"No, we found her like this." Aimée turned to René, who'd knelt beside her. "Tell the *flics* to hurry."

Choking sounds came from Irati. "What do you mean?"

"I heard a car pull away, then saw blood," Aimée said. "Who was in your house, Irati?"

And then she felt Irati's fists punching her. "*Non, non . . .* this can't happen!"

Aimée caught her arms and pulled her away. "Let's go inside."

Irati shook Aimée's hands off. "And leave her in the cold?"

Aimée noticed the snapped twigs, bent bushes, the flattened grass feathering the gravel. She saw damp footprints and something that glinted.

"Please. I'm sorry, but it's better if we don't touch anything."

Before she could check the bushes, a thump came from behind her and Irati sprawled, collapsed, sobbing on the dirt.

* * *

AIMÉE PACED IN the closet-sized upstairs sitting room. Twenty minutes, stuck in here, after giving her statement. Her heart ached for Morbier. His phone didn't answer.

Below, flashing blue and red lights bathed the townhouse in an eerie glow. In the rear, bright white lights set up at the crime scene painted the back in stark detail. Xavierre's body had been removed; *le Proc,* the prosecutor, had come and gone; technicians in jumpsuits had finished combing the gravel, the bushes, the stone wall. One by one the lights shut off, and the crew packed their crime-scene kits.

Already? She opened the latticed window, breathed in the

frigid damp air. Snatches of conversation rose from the terrace: ". . . classify a crime scene by what it tells me. This shows low planning, high passion, as opposed to high planning, low emotion."

Footsteps. The door opened and Lieutenant Hénard, the middle-aged, angular-jawed duty *flic*, entered. One look at the window and he shut it and pulled the velvet drapes. He sat down at the escritoire on a gilded chair too small for his large frame. Aimée expected it to snap.

"Sit down, Mademoiselle," he said.

"Did you find the wounded person?"

"Mademoiselle, I need a clarification of your statement." Hénard didn't look up from his notes.

"But he or she can't have gotten far," she said. "The blood on the gravel—"

"We're handling this investigation, Mademoiselle," Hénard interrupted, consulting another page in his notebook.

She'd almost welcome a cocky Brigade Criminelle high-ranking detective to question her instead of this by-the-book plodder. His pen scratched over the paper.

"Mademoiselle Leduc, please explain those bruises on your arm."

"But I told you," she said. "You have my credentials."

Hénard pushed Aimée's PI license, with its less-than-flattering photo of her, across the polished desk.

"*Merci*, but of course you realize it's in your interest to cooperate."

"Lieutenant Hénard, I already explained," she said, tapping her heels. "Poor Irati went into shock. Denial, anger I think, but she lashed out as I tried to calm her. I wanted to remove her from her mother and not disturb the scene. Ask her."

Hénard consulted his notes. "In shock, yes. She had trouble calming down enough to answer all our questions. The police psychologist sedated her."

"Of course my colleague, René Friant, confirmed my account." She stretched out her arms. "Look, do you see any scratches, marks other than a bruise? Xavierre fought her assailant, her fingernails were broken. But there was no blood on her. What about the half-dried blood spatters on the gravel? The figure I mentioned standing at the window?"

He snapped his notebook shut with a sour look. "We're quite aware, Mademoiselle. That's all for now."

Shutting her out, standard police procedure. "Have you notified Commissaire Morbier yet?"

"Command handles notification."

"He's my godfather." She leaned forward. "If there's any possible way I could speak with him. You know, coming from me—"

"Noted, Mademoiselle," he interrupted. "Now join the officer in the other room."

In other words, go home. Typical. Stonewall a witness after taking his statement.

"But you're questioning the guests who'd attended the party, the caterers?"

"Let the professionals do their work, Mademoiselle," Hénard said, an edge to his voice.

She wanted to tear the notebook from his hand, read his notes. Instead, she smiled. "My father was a *flic*; I'm acquainted with—"

"This way, Mademoiselle." He cut her off, opened the door, and gestured downstairs.

In the dining room, Irati's wedding banner still hung from the ceiling. Aimée's heart caught. Now, instead of a marriage, it would be a funeral. The cherries had congealed on the plate of *gâteau* Basque.

She excused herself to use the bathroom in the hall. Inside, she paused until she heard retreating footsteps, then climbed on the marble bidet's rim. She opened the tall bathroom window to the terrace. Still in conversation, the inspector was huddled with a crime-scene technician. The technician was smoking; a plume of gray smoke rose, lazed, then dissipated in the night.

"Called to a case like this last night," the tech said. "Classic signs."

"Coming to conclusions already?" the inspector said.

"A beautiful woman strangled with her own scarf?" He paused. "It's a common scenario. Her man's jealous, reason clouded by anger. They fight, it gets out of hand. An hour later, drunk, full of remorse, he confesses." He paused. "Crime of passion. In theory, of course."

"Says who?" said the inspector.

"The *mec* left evidence," he said. "They always do."

"Circumstantial," the inspector said. "Unless you convince *le Proc* otherwise."

"You call the item we found embedded in fresh footprints circumstantial?" A pause. "I hate to say it, but this one's not good news." His voice drifted away.

She tiptoed forward on the bidet, teetering on the edge. The gloved crime-scene technician moistened his thumb and forefinger, then tamped his cigarette out between his fingers, stuck the butt in his pocket, and shot a look at his team. "We found this. It must have been dislodged in the struggle."

"Got his name on it, then?" a voice said. "Handy, eh? We can go home."

That quick? Was it what she'd seen glinting in the dirt?

Loud knocking erupted on the bathroom door. "Mademoiselle Leduc?"

She stepped down, flushed the toilet, and looked in the mirror to tame a stray eyebrow. She tried to calm the trembling in her hands.

In the hallway, a blue-uniformed *flic* guided her to the kitchen, a remodeled state-of-the-art wall-to-wall marble affair. "We'll contact you for further questioning if needed."

She bit her lip, wondering about the item discovered by the crime-scene tech. "Do you know if there's a suspect?"

No expression showed on his face.

"But the footprints outside, that would explain—"

"And I explained to you," he interrupted, "exit through the kitchen."

The *flics* were barking up the wrong tree. She felt it in her bones.

Family photos were pinned on the corkboard by the kitchen pantry. She paused, saddened at the snapshots of Xavierre and Irati in happy times at the beach in what looked like the Basque countryside, with sheep and snow-tipped mountains. She glanced behind her. The *flic's* back was turned. She unpinned the best photo, one of Irati smiling and Xavierre taking a picnic basket from the trunk of a car, and slipped it into her pocket.

A bruised night sky hovered above the walled driveway. Cloud wisps obscured the moon. The cold air seared her lungs. Still shaken, she pulled her coat tighter.

"Such a tragedy," René said outside on the gravel, shaking his head. "Let's go. My body's numb. You look cold."

She surveyed the driveway, the back gate. "Did you notice a catering truck when we arrived?"

René shook his head.

"Neither did I." She paused. "Something's different."

An empty space lay ahead of a dark maroon two-seater Mercedes coupe. "Another Mercedes was parked here, remember?"

René stomped his feet in the cold, nodding, interest in his eyes. "That's right. Sedan. Nice model, too."

She glanced at the window, pulled the photo from her pocket. She stared at it, then showed René. "Like the one in this photo?"

René nodded.

She ran over to the *flic*, who was now striding ahead to a waiting police car. He was speaking into the microphone clipped to his collar.

"Officer, may I speak with Hénard?"

"Hénard's gone. We've been called to an incident, Mademoiselle."

"Another Mercedes was parked here." She pointed to the tire tracks.

"A priority call. But we have your statement, Mademoiselle," he said, static erupting from his collar microphone.

"But you don't understand. I think this car—"

"The crime-scene technicians examined the area, Mademoiselle." Blue lights flashing, siren whining, his car shot over the gravel and out the driveway.

\* \* \*

"WHAT A RATS' nest, Aimée," René said, gunning the Citroën into the narrow lane. "Poor Morbier."

Sadness weighted her down, thinking of her godfather hearing the news via officialdom.

René hit the brakes as a cat, a charcoal shadow, streaked across the street. He downshifted into second and hit the horn, turned the corner, and sped up.

"Don't you think it's better if the news comes from you?"

She took a deep breath and tried Morbier's number again.

"No answer, René."

"Give it a few minutes. You need to explain what we saw. He'll know what to do."

She was prepared to do just that, but for a couple of small problems: his phone didn't answer; he was in Lyon. And he'd enlisted her help; he'd suspected something.

She cleared her throat. "Of course, but that missing Mercedes. . . ." She sucked in her lip. "I heard it pull away."

"Me, too." René nodded. "A diesel with a knock, right before you found Xavierre. I know what you're thinking. But would the murderer be stupid enough to steal the car and think it wouldn't be traced? That Irati wouldn't notice?"

She needed to think about that.

"That is, if the murderer took it," René said. "Doubtful."

"No harm in finding out, René."

"What can you do, Aimée?" René stopped at a red light. "Trace the car?"

"Not officially. The *flics* made it clear they don't appreciate interference." But with a little charm and luck, she could. "Take a right." She switched on the interior light, reapplying her lipstick in the visor mirror, and dabbed Chanel No. 5 on her nearest pulse points.

René shook his head.

"Any other ideas, René?" She snapped the compact shut. "I'm playing it by the—"

"Hem of your skirt. Like usual, Aimée."

He shifted into first. She saw the set of René's jaw. His white-knuckled hands on the steering wheel. "What's wrong?"

"Xavierre's Basque, *non*?" He checked the rearview mirror. "Last week in Biarritz a Basque was murdered after church, right in front of his family. Some ten-year-old vendetta."

Another angle to consider? "Nothing points to politics here, unless I'm missing something."

"*Everything's* political with the Basques. Murdering tourists on the Costa Brava is their specialty." René pounded his fist on the steering wheel. "Like my cousin. He was fifteen, on a school holiday on the Costa Brava, when a bomb ripped his bus apart."

She'd had no idea. "I'm so sorry."

"'Sorry' doesn't bring him back," René said.

"You never told me. But that's ETA, the Basque terrorists," she said. "Pull over there."

She pointed to the small, storefront-like Commissariat de Police across from the darkened Marché de Passy, the indoor market. The Commissariat, a vestige of the old neighborhood, had a blue, white, and red flag whipping in the wind in front of it and a plaque on the light blue door. This remnant of the former village faced the market, not the designer shops and haunts of the wealthy.

René exhaled. "I don't get it. Didn't you already give a statement to the *flics*?"

She nodded, combing her fingers through the blond streaks wisping behind her ear.

"Yet we're parked in front of the Commissariat and nothing else looks open." René pulled on the parking brake.

Outside the car window, a figure walked by on the pavement. Alert, she watched. Only an older man, his cap low on his head, wearing a long wool coat, walking his dog, pausing every so often by the gutter. Otherwise, the street lay deserted.

"Time's crucial," she said. "Investigational red tape bogs everything down. Filing crime-scene reports can take up to twelve hours. I need to know whether the missing car's important or not."

She hoped she sounded more confident than she felt, that he didn't notice the trembling in her knees.

The Mercedes. She had to find the Mercedes. An hour and a half head start, and the *flic* hadn't even listened to her or noted it down. Irati wouldn't notice that the car was missing until too late.

"Irati's under sedation," she said. "When she wakes, she'll be desperate. Frantic."

"*Exactement,*" René said. "Who wouldn't be? A daughter losing her mother. . . ."

She felt the buried pain in her heart. That little pain that never went away. Aimée's American mother had abandoned her when she was eight years old.

René averted his gaze. "My turn for sorry." His mouth tightened.

She smiled and touched his hand. "It's all in the timing."

"Timing? How?"

She shouldered her bag. "I don't know yet." She reached for the door handle. "But I'll find out."

She paused and caught his hangdog look. His pale face.

"Your hip bothering you, again? What's wrong?"

"What's *right,* Aimée?"

The windows fogged, and he hit the defroster.

"This murder. Morbier," he went on. "But I worry about you," he said, "that you'll get involved just as you're recovering your health." René turned on the defroster full-blast. "Not that worrying does any good."

She shuddered. This was the last thing she wanted, with a business to run, ongoing projects, clients, and pending proposals. She'd just spent a month on her back, and she needed to catch up. "Did I go looking for this?"

"Xavierre's murder's not your fault, or your responsibility," René said.

"But I owe Morbier," she said, biting her lip. "I failed."

"Failed? She kicked us out, remember?" René said. "It's more important for you to support Morbier in his grief."

She nodded. But if she didn't track down this car, do something, she'd get no sleep.

"'In the river of life,' as Saj says, 'all things merge,'" René said.

"And that makes it easy?" she said. "Have you heard from him yet?"

Saj, their part-time hacker, had gone on a well-earned vacation: a meditation retreat in southern India.

"He's at the ashram in Pondicherry, as far as I know. He won't respond to e-mail during meditation courses." René's clenched fists gripped the steering wheel. A faint sheen of perspiration showed on his face.

Best to keep his mind off what had happened. She remembered him in the hospital, how she'd almost lost him. Never again. "With Saj away, you need to check the data sniffer feed, René."

"For once, you're being practical?"

She twisted the leather strap of her bag. "Don't you need to prepare?" She squeezed his hand. "I know you, René."

"You do?"

The atmosphere became grave. For a moment she couldn't read his expression. But she couldn't think about that now. She had things to do. She opened the car door. "Places to go, René."

And miles before I sleep, she thought, keeping her trembling hands in her pockets as she traversed the zebra-striped crosswalk.

* * *

"36 85 RS 75." Aimée read the Mercedes license plate number from the photo in her hand. A smiling Xavierre and Irati posed with a red-and-white picnic basket and rolling hills in the background. "A maroon Mercedes sedan, say two years old. Diesel."

"You don't ask much, do you, Mademoiselle Aimée?" Thesset cleared his throat. "Me, here in the Commissariat with two men, two others out responding to calls. Do you think I've got nothing to do?"

Thesset was approaching his mid-fifties. A career *flic* who'd graduated from the Police Academy with her father and Morbier, now edging toward retirement in the Commissariat, mostly preoccupied with disturbances of the peace or robbery by a disgruntled servant.

"Looks quiet to me, Thesset."

"Heated up tonight," he said. "Murder of some *haute bourgeoise* matron. They're calling it a crime of passion. Shows you never can tell what's going on behind the gilded doors."

Her shoulders tensed. Not good. It sounded like the crime-scene techs wanted to go home early, shelve the investigation to low priority, and discount other motives.

But she'd worry about that later. The timing between the car pulling away and Xavierre's murder wasn't a coincidence. She needed Thesset to trace the car before he or the investigators finally connected the dots tomorrow.

"Crime of passion sounds convenient," she said.

"More like they wanted to warm their *derrières*." Thesset shrugged.

"Any leads yet?" she asked offhand.

"Not my call. Or my turf."

A twinge of guilt passed through her. Here she held a photo of the dead woman in her hand. But Thesset could search without making an official report. And if she'd jumped to conclusions, say the old couple at the party had borrowed the Mercedes, no one would be the wiser. No harm done. No record.

"I'm not supposed to do this, you know."

"But you're the pro, Thesset."

Thesset's expertise lay in navigating *Système D*, the catchall term for getting things done. He was efficient behind the thick-lensed gray-framed glasses mounted on his beaklike nose, his misleading sallow jowls and permanent squint. "Like a pigeon," she'd once said to her father at the Commissariat, and he'd put a finger over his mouth. "*Shhh*. We call him that, but never to his face."

"*S'il vous plaît*, Thesset. I'm asking on behalf of Morbier."

She heard the fax machine come to life behind the wooden partition, tried to ignore the acrid cigarette smoke spiraling from the ashtray on the counter, the empty pack of Mentos crumpled near the phone.

"Let the old coot request this himself."

"*Très compliqué,* Thesset." She leaned forward as if in confidence. "A delicate situation, if you know what I mean. Morbier's lady friend's daughter fell in with a bad sort—a vindictive type. Now he's her ex and out on parole. He took her Mercedes tonight. The daughter wants nothing to do with him, no accusations, just her car back. No urge to make a report and land him back in prison and deal with recriminations on his release. *Compris?* A small favor, Morbier said. He counted on you keeping it quiet. Unofficial."

"Sounds like a soap opera," Thesset said.

She wished it were, but figured it wouldn't be the first time he'd gotten a request to keep *haut bourgeois* linen clean.

"Me, I've got work to do," Thesset said. "Tell Morbier to get on it himself."

"*Mais,* Morbier's in Lyon." She expelled air from her mouth. Tried to look helpless and without a clue. Not hard. "Some big investigation," she said, playing it to the hilt. "I don't know what, but he asked for my help."

Thesset squinted behind his glasses. Put down his pen.

"Lyon? That circus?" A cough, then he cleared his throat again. "Better him than me."

What did that mean?

"*Et alors,* in that case," Thesset said, "I'll see what I can do."

The change in Thesset's attitude intrigued her. "What's happening in Lyon?"

"Nothing I want to know about." He shrugged.

She left it for now and flashed a big smile. "Then how about a trace through traffic division? The patrol cars in Bois de Boulogne, little things, the usual."

"Usual?" He snorted. "If you weren't taller than me now, I'd take you on my lap, like I used to, and tickle behind your knees."

She'd loved that. "And give me the hiccups."

"Like I said, you don't want much, do you?" A sigh. "I'll put the alert out to my boys on patrol."

"How long will it take, Thesset?"

"To find the car?" He shrugged. "Two minutes, two hours, two days. Depends."

The murderer could have abandoned the car. But casting a wide net, a maxim on the force, would find it sooner or later. Regular patrols cruised the neighboring Bois de Boulogne, a stretch of forest double the size of New York's Central Park. The big lung of Paris, locals called it, a park honeycombed with roads, horse trails, the Longchamp racing course, and also Brazilian transvestites offering their services on the fringes, a frequent issue with the consular staff of the numerous embassies dotting the 16th arrondissement. YOU PLAY, YOU PAY, headlined a recent scandal sheet over a transvestite's blackmail demand, complete with compromising photos. Immediately hushed up while the junior consul was packed off to his home country.

She wished her shoulders weren't aching with fatigue. And that she could provoke Thesset into revealing some details about "the Lyon circus."

"Morbier promised he'd return tonight," she said, hating to lie.

"Don't count on it," he said. "Between you and me, Mademoiselle Aimée, who knows. It's three branches all jockeying for credit. A mess."

"Anything to do with the news on the radio?"

"*Salauds* killed a *flic*. And you know what that means."

A priority. All forces would be centered on a policeman's killing.

"Morbier's a Commissaire Divisionnaire now; Lyon's not his turf."

"It's not for me to say." Thesset's eyes suddenly seemed shuttered. He was holding something back. Impatient, she tapped her nails on the police blotter and noticed a chip on her newly lacquered pinkie.

Thesset's jaw tightened. Papers rustled from behind the partition, a filing-cabinet drawer shut. She shivered in the cold unheated reception area at the scuffed wood counter.

"Aaah. But on the radio." She thought for a moment trying to draw him out. "Those roadblocks? *Bon,* what can you tell me?"

"Every branch's salivating to get the *flic*-killer, that's all I know." Thesset pounded his fist on the counter. "The *flic's* wife's eight months pregnant. Poor thing."

Sad. No doubt the *flics* were seeking vengeance. With all forces concentrating on the murder of one of their own, she realized, Xavierre's murderer could slip under their radar.

Through the open door in the rear office, she saw a blue-uniformed *flic* pull a fax from the printer. "Thesset, look at this."

"I'll ring you later," she said. "*Et merci,* Thesset."

Aimée snapped her bag shut. Thesset disappeared into the office. She paused behind the divider, her ear to the smudged glass, and overheard "damned ETA terrorists . . . acting up again."

Then the door closed.

\* \* \*

ETA, THE BASQUE Nationalists. Xavierre was Basque. Was there a connection? Had that worried Morbier?

The street lay quiet, apart from water rushing in the gutter. Typical of the staid *quartier*: not even a café open. But a perfect *quartier* for terrorists to hide in, in a tony residential district where everyone minded their own business. And never a taxi when you needed one, she thought, scanning the empty street. She shouldered her bag, her only companions a streetlight and the low, distant moan of a cat in heat.

Around the corner, a lone taxi paused at the intersection. Thank god. She caught it before the light changed.

"Île Saint-Louis, *s'il vous plaît*," she said, giving her address, and popped her last two Doliprane aspirin, dry-mouthed, in the back seat. Fifteen minutes later, she punched in the digicode of her building, a seventeenth-century soot-stained townhouse on the quai, and stepped into the cobbled courtyard. Beyond the ancient pear tree, she noticed with relief, the windows in her concierge's loge were lit.

"Late and breathless," frowned Madame Cachou, her concierge. "As usual."

Aimée leaned down to pet Miles Davis, her bichon frisé. His wet nose sniffed her ankles. "*Désolée*, Madame. Work. Traffic." Murder, but she left that out.

"Good thing!" said Madame Cachou. "With my bursitis, I can't walk Miles Davis up and down three times a day."

Madame Cachou, a chronic complainer, was growing worse in her old age. Framed in the doorway of her loge in the courtyard, Madame handed Aimée the leash from the wall hook. Miles Davis emitted a low growl, which reminded Aimée of her shoes, the dog poo.

"*Un moment,*" Madame Cachou said. "There's a package for you."

Warmth emanated from Madame Cachou's loge, a steaming cup by an armchair near the *télé* showing the late-night France2 news. Aimée's tired body ached and she couldn't wait to get under the duvet. An announcer spoke as a scene flashed on the screen: dark sky punctuated by lights, yellow crime-scene tape, a narrow lane bordered by high walls. Her shoulders tightened. She recognized those stone walls. The walls of Xavierre's garden.

"The Police Judiciaire refused to issue a statement regarding the murdered ex-wife of a prominent attorney found tonight in her bedroom in the 16th arrondissement."

*Bedroom?* She dropped Miles Davis's leash.

"Sources close to the investigation revealed that attention is being focused on the victim's relationship, referring to it as a crime of passion. The source indicated that a suspect was about to be detained."

*Crime of passion?* The hair rose on the back of her neck. The media and the *flics* had gotten it all wrong.

"Last time," Madame Cachou said. "Building regulations don't permit receiving business correspondence here, Mademoiselle." She pointed to a yellowed paper of building regulations as she handed Aimée a Frexpresse package.

Always a stickler for rules, her concierge. Aimée glanced at the return address. Infologic. Work-related files she could handle tomorrow.

"I bent the rules, but . . . ," said Madame Cachou, "seeing as you're recovered, fit, and back at work, no more."

She wished she felt fit instead of exhausted. More worry lodged in her head over this turn of events with respect to Xavierre. The pain of telling Morbier . . . but he certainly must already know by now.

She trudged up the worn marble stairs to her door. Darkness, a chill, and rising damp from the Seine outside met her in her empty apartment. She kicked the radiator. Then again, until it sputtered to life. She hung up her faux fur, tossed the Frexpresse package on the hall table with her bag, and wedged off her heels. Miles Davis pawed at them. "Not this pair, furball."

She picked them up. A dark brown-maroon blotch stained the candy-red insole. Ruined. She'd never get the blood out.

And then it struck her, piercing the fog of tiredness in her mind: she was holding the proof right in her hand. The killer's blood. Her spine stiffened. She took a plastic baggie from the hall escritoire drawer, slipping her high heels inside. "They go straight to the lab in the morning. Good call, furball."

*Tuesday Morning*

MORBIER'S TOBACCO-STAINED FINGERS trembled as he lit his second Gauloise. Why couldn't he feel numb? Numb like the victims' families he'd broken the same news to countless times, more times than he liked to remember. And he remembered every one. Their shocked faces: ". . . but it can't be"; then his words sinking in. The collapse into tears.

Why didn't he even feel anger, hurt, grief? Instead he floated, as if out of his body. His mind blurred when he should be analyzing Xavierre's last words, rethinking her every action.

There was so much to do, so many facets to consider in the investigation, so much to concentrate on: the crime-scene results, lab tests, questioning the family, any witnesses, speaking with Aimée. But here he was, spinning his wheels, waiting in the Préfecture's office for Suffren. The last person he wanted to talk to. Now or ever. Suffren's office afforded a view of the green-brown Seine. Not a corner office, but a sign of the favor he'd attained in the six years since Morbier had almost sidetracked his career.

The longer Suffren kept him waiting, the more he wondered at the abrupt summons that had taken him from the Morgue, wishing that his last view of Xavierre hadn't been her wide red-veined eyes, her delicate neck red and bruised as she lay on the stainless-steel morgue table; that the creeping feeling of helplessness would subside; that he could do something to bring the smile back on—

The door creaked open and Suffren, a man in his early forties, whip-thin, brunette with a stripe of white hair showing above his ears, gestured for Morbier to sit down. Suffren kept his cell phone glued to his ear, emitting occasional hmms and grunts. Only once did he look up and give a small apologetic shrug.

*Upstart, out to prove himself, has a chip on his shoulder* were the comments Morbier recalled from Suffren's file. Morbier's review team, singularly unimpressed by Suffren, had passed on his application based on his low scores on the officer examination.

If Morbier remembered this, no doubt Suffren remembered with venom. Morbier settled in the upright wooden chair, wishing he could go to the crime lab. He tried to push that aside, get the interview over with, a formality. He needed to channel his nervous energy into the anger he knew would come . . . so as to find out who'd done this.

Suffren hung up the phone and studied the view outside his window for a moment. In the pale lemon morning light, a lone seagull squawked on the quai and clouds floated over the jagged Left Bank rooftops.

"Commissaire," Suffren said, leaning forward, tenting his fingers. "You had a known relationship with the victim. Physical evidence found. . . ."

"*Oui*, of course, I do . . . did." Morbier leaned forward. "You're handling the investigation?"

"That thing of yours for the ladies, eh? I remember . . . didn't your Arab mistress, one of them . . . I forget, die in Marseilles?"

Insult, inference, intimidation, Morbier knew well the standard interrogation techniques. He used them himself. Determined, he steeled his nerves to get this questioning over with so the investigation could proceed.

"Mouna left me years ago," he said. "Two years later, she was caught in crossfire in the Belleville riots."

"It's coming back, yes, Mouna," Suffren said, flexing his tented fingers, his voice layered with innuendo. "Her daughter Samia was murdered not much later in Belleville, in 1994."

"*Our* daughter," Morbier interrupted. His fists clenched in his corduroy jacket pocket.

"A brutal slaying, if I remember. And your grandson. . . ."

"Marc lives in Morocco with his paternal grandparents."

Morbier balled the handkerchief in his pocket.

"Quite a protracted custody battle over little Marc, *non?* Allegations surfaced concerning . . ." he paused. "Abuse, I think."

"Get your information correct, Suffren. There was no abuse. His Muslim grandparents alleged religious and educational discrimination." Morbier kept his breathing steady with effort. "I paid Marc's Catholic school tuition instead of sending him to the mosque school. The court threw the case out. But in another legal round, well, two grandparents beats one." Morbier kept his gaze steady. "But you know all this; it's in the open file on your desk."

"Murder follows the ones you love, *non,* Morbier?"

Suffren was wasting no time, Morbier thought. So he'd descend to his level and get right to it.

"Maybe you think it's clever to knit these incidents together," Morbier said, "but they won't make a sweater. My grandson's father was convicted of Samia's murder. He's serving the next twenty years in Clairvaux. Didn't one of *your* new team put him there? Quit wasting time."

"But I'm establishing a pattern, the history over a period of years."

Word for word from the Police Academy textbook. Morbier tapped his worn heel. He'd be bored with this, if it weren't for his underlying unease. His frequent refusals to play police politics over the years had won him more enemies than friends. He kept important players happy and his head down, doing investigations his way. Most of the time. But he realized he'd ticked someone off big-time if it had come to this.

"Either get creative, Suffren, or find a new playbook, but get on with it. Then look for the real killer."

Suffren glanced up. "Creative. That's good. I like that. But you beat me to it. Eh? No TGV ticket record to Lyon; matter of fact, you arrived an hour late . . . enough time to strangle her."

"What?" His shoulders tensed. "You're calling me a suspect?"

"Tell me why you dismissed your driver."

Now it had gotten real, Morbier realized.

"How I run my investigation, that's my business."

"Why hasn't this come up in your notes? Meanwhile, a Lyon investigation team member noted your flustered . . . *non*, pardon, disheveled appearance, and that you turned the team over to the second in command."

Morbier could bluff this out. He had to.

"It was so the investigation could proceed," Morbier said. "I delegated according to the surveillance information received."

"But you were late. Can you account for that time? Where were you?"

Morbier averted his eyes. "Talk to Inspector Laguardiere."

"But I can't, you see; he's on medical leave."

*Merde!* Another hernia operation? His bad back? Laguardiere spent more time in the hospital than out of it.

"*Et alors*, handle it through the usual channels. I understand you've got to rule out people close to Xavierre—"

"But Laguardiere is the proper channel, as you know," Suffren interrupted. "Why don't you reconsider your answer?"

"I can't discuss the ongoing investigation." Morbier shook his head. The fur-like fabric pellets in his corduroy jacket pocket were ground to lint now.

"But we need to establish your whereabouts. Very simple, and much less painful than the alternative."

"Check with Laguardiere. He'll tell you it's—"

"Disturb the man after his heart attack yesterday? With pulmonary thrombosis and surgery scheduled?"

"I'm sorry to hear that. I didn't know." Morbier shrugged. All the old dinosaurs like him were en route to the cemetery. "After his recovery, he'll clear this up." Morbier made to stand. "If that's all?"

Suffren grimaced as if in pain. "If that could only take care of the discrepancy. But I'm afraid this gets in the way." He held a clear plastic evidence bag in his hand. "A Commissaire Divisionnaire–rank tiepin. Serial number on the inside. One of only eight issued in the last few years. Yours, I believe, Commissaire Morbier." He said it with relish.

Morbier stared at the tiepin glinting under the fluorescent light. Then he felt his tie. Gone.

"Looks like mine." Morbier nodded. Where had he dropped this?

"We discovered your tiepin in a muddy footprint close to the victim's body. I believe it will match the worn left heel on your shoe."

"What?" Morbier's jaw clamped tight.

Suffren pressed a button on his intercom. "We're ready."

Two white-coated technicians from the basement laboratory under the Quai des Orfèvres entered the office. He'd played cards with one of them, Desnos, the older and senior in rank, last Friday. Desnos still owed him a hundred francs.

"We're affording you privacy, of course, given your rank," said Suffren. "I'm sure you'll cooperate while they take an impression of your shoe. Undo your shoelaces, *s'il vous plaît*."

Stunned, Morbier leaned forward.

Desnos averted his eyes and set down his metal box labeled PLASTER.

Morbier's jaw spasmed . . . he made himself speak . . . the words came from somewhere. "Under these circumstances—"

"From now on, Commissaire, I caution you to speak only to the legal representative assigned by the Inspecteur Général," Suffren interrupted.

*Inspection Générale des Services*, Internal Affairs, *la Police des Polices*. Most called it *boeuf-et-carottes:* the stew of suspicion a *flic* simmered in while suspended.

Morbier could have sworn he saw a gleam in Suffren's small eyes.

"This is all wrong, Suffren. You don't really want to do this—"

"Escort him to IGS downstairs for interrogation, gentlemen. I believe it's on your way."

*Tuesday Morning*

AIMÉE WOKE UP to the ringing of her cell phone, which was beside her on the duvet. Weak bands of sunlight slanted across the herringbone-patterned wood floor. Rubbing her eyes, she looked at the time. Eight A.M.

Morbier's number showed on caller ID. Finally. She sat up, took a breath, and clicked ANSWER.

"Leduc, why didn't you tell me?" Morbier's hoarse voice came over the line.

"I tried to." A pang of guilt stabbed her. "I'm so sorry, Morbier. When do you return from Lyon?"

She heard clanging noises in the background, like steel treads running over concrete. "I'm at the Préfecture."

"*Bon.* Won't take me ten minutes," she said, sitting up, grabbing her stovepipe jeans from the chair. "Just a moment." Awake now, she put the phone down, slipped her worn cashmere sweater over her head, put the phone back to her ear. "I have things to tell you. Much better in person."

Pause. More clanging. "Not a good time."

"Why?"

Shouts, then a voice came over the line: "Time's up, Commissaire."

"I can't talk, Leduc."

"You're involved in an interrogation?"

"You could say that." Morbier's voice sounded different. Almost resigned.

That fast? "Look, something smelled last night. We need to talk—"

"A little difficult, Leduc," Morbier said. "Since I'm the suspect."

\* \* \*

THE PRÉFECTURE'S VAULTED stone holding cells oozed mildew and rot. Last remodeled during the Terror, if then, Aimée thought as she held Morbier's hand across the gouged wooden table. She felt his thick fingers, the moist ridges of his palm, and squeezed hard.

"Don't worry, Morbier, of course they'll release you at any moment," she said, managing a small smile. "Clear up this horrible mistake on top of—"

"I don't want you involved, Leduc." Stubble dotted Morbier's chin, lines were etched in his brow, and his drooping Basset-hound eyes were pools of pain.

"Xavierre loved you; there was no other man." She squeezed his hand tighter. "She told me you met more than twenty years ago, *a coup de foudre*. You have to know that."

He nodded, but there was a lost look in his eyes. "*Merci*."

Her heart ached at seeing him like this. But they'd fix this mistake any moment. This terrible mistake.

She pushed the bag with a change of clothes and his shaving kit across the table. Handed him *un express* from the machine in a small white plastic cup. "I got this upstairs," she said.

He took a sip. Nodded. "The usual lukewarm brown piss."

His rumpled corduroy jacket and a food stain on the lapel caught her eye. The faint smell of mustard and defeat clung to him.

"We've only got fifteen minutes." She omitted telling him about the four hours it had taken to call his colleagues—numerous—and friends—not as numerous, it turned out—to wangle visitation for her in the *garde à vue*. No one had the "right connections" with Internal Affairs, they said. More likely they were head-in-the-sand afraid, she thought. It sickened her, knowing how Morbier had stuck his neck out for others. Favors oiled the system, her father always said, give and take, like currency but more valuable when your neck sat on the block. Favors conveniently forgotten if you became a pariah. Or had Morbier used up his favors?

In the end, she had opened the cell door by threatening to call the *Libération* journalist known for his recent exposé on police corruption.

"Xavierre was afraid," Aimée said; "your gut told you right. Someone was in the house. I saw blood outside on the gravel, heard a car take off, and found her . . . I'm so sorry, Morbier."

"Nice try, Leduc," he said. His shoulders sagged. "Proof puts me at the scene."

She shook her head in disbelief. "Proof? But you were in Lyon."

Dripping sounds in steady rhythm came from the corner. Morbier looked away. "I was watching Xavierre through the window. I couldn't help myself," he said. "A jealous old fool."

"I don't understand what you're saying." She let go of his hand.

"I was in the garden, Leduc." There was a faint hiss under his breath. "I left my footprints in the mud, and my tieclip."

This couldn't be happening. It didn't make sense.

"What?"

"I saw Xavierre arguing. Shouting, but I couldn't hear. She threw something at a figure. A man. But his back was turned."

She fought welling tears. There was a knot in her stomach.

"What do you mean?"

"Then cars pulled up with arriving guests and I left."

She took a breath. Tried to make sense of it. "Why didn't you tell me?"

"I hoped Xavierre would . . . what good did it do?" Remorse and grief cratered his face. He put his shaking head in his hands.

"*Mais* . . . wait, you'd gone to Xavierre's earlier?"

He nodded.

"What else, Morbier?" A growing doubt nauseated her.

"Don't get involved, Leduc. It's not safe." He looked up, then put his head back in his hands.

"What the hell does that mean, Morbier?" She stood up, took a step, sat down again hard in the chair. Calm, she had to act calm, and rational. Get answers. "What's really wrong, Morbier?"

"I'm too old for this," Morbier said. "Been too old for a long time. Xavierre's gone. Life's gone to hell."

Like a dog kicked too many times, the fight had gone out of him. "Tragic, yes, Morbier. So you spied on her. That doesn't mean anything. My god, *I* saw her alive after that. Your driver, the Lyon team will confirm." She snorted. "Why hasn't this idiotic investigation folded like a pack of cards hours ago?"

But he'd looked up, his gaze following the pipes snaking up the stone wall. An old-fashioned *robinet*, a metal-faced water spout, dripped, leaking a thin silver trickle into the grooved stone gutter. The whole place reeked of damp and wet. The continuous drip, drip got to her.

"That's leaked for twenty years," Morbier said, his voice lowered. "Time someone took care of it."

"Call the plumber," she said, irritated. Why had he given up? "Look, Morbier, you've got to fight this. You've given a lifetime to the force, lived and breathed your work. . . ." She stopped before she said *until Xavierre stepped into your life and gave you a shot at happiness.* Poor man, nothing to look forward to now. "So many years of service. High-profile investigations. Your retirement's coming up."

"All gone up in smoke, Leduc."

Her spine stiffened. "What are they holding over you?"

"Keep your friends close and your enemies closer, they say."

"Meaning?"

"*Désolé*, Leduc. My fault to have involved you." Morbier stood, nodded to the guard. "Forgive me."

Morbier asking *her* forgiveness. Had he ever in his life asked her that?

She jumped up and put her arms around him. Big solid Morbier, the one she depended on. She inhaled his musky scent mingled with tobacco, mustard, and worn corduroy and glanced at the guard. "Who's framing you, Morbier?" she whispered.

His brown eyes flickered. In his gaze, she saw the reflection of the silver pinpricks of dripping water.

"Stay out of this, Leduc. I don't want anything to happen to you." He kissed her on both cheeks, took his bag. "For

An articulate showman: he hit all the right notes, she imagined, for his clients. But she wasn't one.

"A room needs a painting and a view," he said. "That's all. Like our farmhouse."

Well-rehearsed in an earthy, Picasso-esque manner with a weather-beaten face to lend credibility. No wonder it brought him commissions. But he was hiding something.

"I'm French Basque, but you French complicate design with froufrou, rococo. Let the natural lines highlight the inner form, the beauty."

*Forget the art lecture*, she wanted to say. She wasn't in a classroom or about to write a check. And then it hit her: he was giving this speech to stall for time, or to avoid revealing his past connection with Xavierre.

"Monsieur Agustino, if you could listen for a moment—"

"*Non, you* must listen. Understand. It's life, how I breathe, my heritage that makes me—"

"Involved with ETA again?" she interrupted.

He shoved the card back into her hand. Glancing down, she noticed the stubbed flesh where his last two fingers would have been. Amazing that he could still paint masterpieces.

"Watch what you're saying." His voice lowered. "In the old prisons, I went back and carved memorials in the dripping walls, memorials to the fallen," he said. "To both sides—the Guardia Civil, ETA. My soul hurt, still does. For years my work has celebrated the Basque spirit, reconciliation, not violence."

His eyes bore into her. "How do you think I lost these?" He lifted his claw-like hand. "Xavierre knows . . . knew that."

Aimée nodded. "I saw your paintings. Breathing life, speaking to me."

"Then you know art touches more minds and spirits than bombs." His arm trembled. His showman side evaporated. "My heart mourns Xavierre. On the phone with her last night, all I could talk about was my commission. How I needed to paint. Our last words. Well, she said I was too caught up in my art like usual. I'll regret it all my life."

Guilt. But over that?

"But didn't you sense her fear? Did she tell you something?"

"Apart from how selfish I've become?" Agustino gave a small shrug. "The family, this big wedding, the home, it's a religion with Basques. Coward that I am, I can't face Irati now, or any of them."

"Who would murder her, Agustino?"

He made a sign of the cross. "God knows. But I broke our pact," he said. "You see, I failed her in the most important thing to her."

"What pact?"

"Made years ago. To be there for each other. I couldn't even do a simple thing, attend her party. And I'd promised to come." He looked away.

"Then this pact's deep, *non?*" she said, trying a guess. "What about the others from your student days in Bayonne? The protestors?"

He turned, his shoulders slumped. But he hadn't answered her question.

"Haven't you maintained the bonds you made with them?" she said. "Like with Xavierre."

"Time takes people away."

"Not the past," she said. "What if the past connects to Xavierre's murder?"

"All those people went to prison." A sigh frosted the air. "Like my brother."

"Look, I tried to talk to Xavierre last night," she said. "To find out if something was wrong. My turn to feel guilt. I couldn't even do that."

"You take your job to heart, Mademoiselle. I respect that."

"Not a job," she said. "A promise I made. A deep debt I owe to a person close to me."

If none of her other words got through to him, she sensed these would.

"You see, Agustino," she said, "I've already made one mistake. If I'd known the trouble Xavierre was in. . . ."

"Giving one's word. . . ." He spoke as if to himself, shaking his head. "But what if you gave it long ago and now it goes against everything you know is right, that you believe in?"

And she thought she understood. "Ask yourself this. Haven't hundreds of innocent people been killed in ETA actions? As you asked me yourself, will killing more people help the Basque movement?"

A flicker of his eyelid.

She pursued it. "There's ways to keep your word and yet help me without saying a thing."

Agustino stood dead still. A long moment passed. Then a little shake of his head.

He closed the door to his atelier. One light went on, a dim glow in the dark valley of green. Only afternoon sounds, the soft cooing of pigeons, a siren's distant wail, could be heard. Not only was he a sad man scarred by regrets, but he was also hiding something. She slipped her card back under the door.

\* \* \*

RUBBING HER COLD hands together, Aimée shivered in the *allée* overhung with chestnut trees near Xavierre's high wall. She turned the corner. Xavierre's neighbor's window provided a view of the back garden and the driveway. This woman, Madame de Boucher—a busybody, according to the concierge—had been born in the building, had lived here eighty years. Aimée mounted the building staircase hoping for a font of information.

"My neighbor's comings and goings?" Madame de Boucher leaned on her ebony walking stick and gave a dismissive wave with her other blue-veined hand. "Ask the concierge."

"But I did, Madame, and she suggested I speak with you." Aimée gave a wide smile and flashed her PI license with the less-than-flattering photo. In the background she heard high-pitched singing and recognized "Leaves of Autumn," based on the Verlaine poem.

"I spoke to the *flics* already," the old woman said. "Told them like I'm telling you, I saw nothing, heard nothing. *C'est tout.*"

Aimée groaned inside. After Agustino, for the past two hours she'd questioned the lane's inhabitants: a retired professor, a musician, several cleaning women and maids, all of whom had said the same thing. People either hadn't been home last night or had drawn their shades. She'd hit another wall.

"A shame, Madame." Arms weary, she set her bag down. "The family's devastated that they can't even hold a service, but I thought—"

"Is that for me?" interrupted Madame de Boucher, staring at the *gâteau* Basque on top, which was emanating a fragrance of cherries.

Aimée saw a way in the door. "Of course, but let me heat it up. Seeing as you've got a. . . ." She paused. Was it a recital? Singing lessons? "There's plenty for your guest."

"Guest?" Then a look of understanding on the old woman's face, crinkling in a web of fine lines. "You mean Hector? I'm busy cleaning, Mademoiselle."

At her age? And in this *quartier* resplendent with hired help?

"Come back tomorrow, Mademoiselle."

She had to get inside in the door.

"But I can help and warm this for you in the kitchen."

"*Comme ça?* In that outfit?"

So her standby funeral suit, a flea-market-find black wool Givenchy, would go to the dry cleaners. "No problem, Madame."

Madame de Boucher tapped her stick on the newspapers piled on the threadbare hall carpet runner. Another wave of her hand. "Into the parlor, then, *s'il vous plaît*."

Humor her, Aimée thought: she might know a detail, might have noticed something over the past few days. Aimée scooped up the rustling, yellowed newspapers and followed Madame de Boucher.

The cracked leather-bound volumes filling a wall of bookshelves and worn, brocaded Louis chairs couldn't mask the faded charm of the nineteenth-century parlor. A chandelier with missing crystals cast a dim glow on the high-ceilinged, carved-wood *boiseries* bordering the cream wood-paneled walls and dried flower arrangements under glass globes.

She felt like she'd entered a Proust novel. Except for the chrome high-tech medic alert remote-control device and the blue-and-yellow-plumed singing parrot perched near a matching cloisonné vase on a claw-footed table.

"Hector's particular, you know," Madame said, pointing to the dirty wire cage.

The parrot's repetitive singing grated on Aimée's ears. She set the *gâteau* Basque down on the table.

"He's my companion of twenty-five years now," she said.

Aimée's nose crinkled as she pulled out the birdcage tray clumped with bird feces dotted with feather fluff. Slants of light from the window lit the faded Turkish carpet, turning it a dull red, reminding her of old blood.

She changed the newspaper lining and jerked her chin toward the window. "What a wonderful view over the garden." She paused, pretending to put it together. "That's Xavierre's garden, *non*?"

"They use it like a parking lot these days. Disgusting."

Aimée nodded. "Of course you notice the comings and goings. How can you miss seeing, eh? Especially last night, Irati's big party, the noise, guests. . . ."

"My stupid cousin widened the gate. In my grandfather's time it was just wide enough for a *fiacre*."

A horse-drawn carriage from the last century.

"Nowadays they're garages," she continued.

"I suppose you knew Madame Xavierre?"

"What's it to you?" The old woman bristled, her tone changed.

Bad tactic. "Madame, I'm—"

"Snooping and asking questions, like they did," Madame de Boucher interrupted.

Aimée's ears perked up. The parrot's tone shrilled. She shoved the clean newspaper-lined tray back inside the cage and tried not to sneeze. If only the damned bird would shut up.

"Who do you mean, Madame?"

"I told them nothing, you understand. Like always."

"But weren't you worried? Upset? Your neighbor's murdered in her garden almost outside your window?" She tried to keep her voice level.

"*Et alors*, I heard nothing." Madame de Boucher's mouth tightened.

"Help me understand the timeline, Madame," she said. "The

report places the murder at seven forty-five. A Mercedes pulled out of that driveway minutes later. Did you hear—"

"The Bomb could drop while I listen to my program on Radio Classique and I wouldn't hear it," Madame de Boucher interrupted. "I knew the poor woman to say '*Bonjour*' in the morning, that's all."

Disappointed, Aimée knew she needed to change tactics. This woman, who'd lived here eighty years, had to know something. And didn't like the *flics*.

"But it's a person like you, Madame, who knows the *quartier*, the rhythm of life here, who can help me the most." She smiled, determined to ingratiate herself. "So quiet and peaceful here."

Madame de Boucher snorted. "*C'est un village ici.*"

Aimée nodded. "*Bien sûr.* Maybe you noticed a person you hadn't seen before in the past few days?"

Madame de Boucher guided Hector, now perched on her ebony stick, into the cleaned cage. With one hand she covered the cage with a black flannel cloth, and the parrot quieted at once. She sighed, sinking into the armchair brocaded with fleurs-de-lis, setting her stick against the armrest.

"A detective?" said Madame de Boucher, her eyes hooded with suspicion, glaring at Aimée's suit. "Since when do the *flics* wear couture? Or do my taxes pay for that?"

Aimée didn't bother to enlighten Madame as to the fact that private detectives didn't work for the *flics*. And wished she had a tissue to wipe off the grit clinging to her hands.

"On my salary I shop at Réciproque, the *dépôt-vente* consignment shop, Madame." Aimée winked. That store was the *quartier*'s bargain-hunter mecca of gently worn couture from wives who cleaned out their closets every season.

"You're some special investigator?" she said, still suspicious.

Aimée sat down. The chair leg creaked under her. "Nothing so exciting, I'm afraid." She leaned forward as if in confidence. "You've heard of Internal Affairs?"

Madame de Boucher shook her head.

"*La police des polices*. We check irregularities in police investigations. But that's between you and me."

"You're all the same. Lists. Always lists," said Madame de Boucher, waving her hand. "We just follow the directives and go by the list, they said."

What did a list have to do with Xavierre's murder?

"Madame, what list?"

"Nineteen forty-three, the hottest July I can remember," she said. The old woman's gaze leveled somewhere in the distance. A past Aimée couldn't see.

"Beat the record," Madame said. "Humid like a steam room. Not even a breeze. I'd closed the shutters, but that didn't keep out the heat. At six A.M. they came pounding on the door. Within two hours they'd ransacked our building, looted every apartment."

Aimée opened her mouth to speak, but Madame de Boucher continued.

"The Milice, the French Gestapo, arrested my brother. Criminals, all of them. Felons released from prison to do the dirty work."

Madame gave a little shrug. "More Nazis lived here than in any other *quartier*. Six hundred ninety-two official German-requisitioned buildings, according to surviving records," she said. "They lusted after the town houses, made the Hotel Majestic a *Kommandantur*. Forbade us calling them *boches*, preferred *Fritz*. Regardless of what we called them, *les Fritz* requisitioned whatever they wanted. Apartments, *hôtels particuliers*, garages, hotels, clinics, bars, restos, theaters. Four Gestapo bureaus, even a *soldatenheim* on the Champs-Elysées."

"But Madame," Aimée interrupted.

"They had taste, I'll say that for them." The old woman continued as if she hadn't heard. "After Liberation, I had to share this apartment with the family of a Milicien who took my brother. Can you imagine?"

Aimée shook her head, hoping this was leading somewhere.

"That too went according to a list. A housing-shortage list. I got a pittance after the war. A few pieces. That one."

She gestured to the blue-and-white cloisonné vase.

"The Milice forced my brother to work in the Bassano, a *hôtel particulier*, outfitted like a restoration studio but an internment camp," she said. "Just blocks away. Who knows now, eh? He restored the looted pianos stored under the Palais de Chaillot. Pleyels, Bechsteins, Steinways, all confiscated from Jewish apartments." A shuttered look crossed her eyes. "Took Madame Morgenstern's baby grand. She lived on the second floor. Later, they took her."

Impatient, Aimée wondered how this connected to Xavierre— or if it even did. Was it just another sad reminiscence of the war by an old woman who kept a parrot for company, death taking everything but her stories? Or had Xavierre's murder jogged loose the old stories, some with a parallel to the present? She had to draw Madame from the past, discover some detail from this eagle-eyed woman who, she suspected, didn't miss a thing.

"So the man, or men, you spoke to wore uniforms?"

"Uniforms?" The old woman shook her head. "They wanted to rent space for their car."

Aimée contained her frustration. The woman dipped back

and forth in time. Not that this was leading anywhere. But she had to try.

"Was that before or after Xavierre's murder?"

"Everything's political, you know."

What did *that* mean? Aimée gritted her teeth. But she nodded, determined to persist.

"You're a Socialist, Madame?"

"Picasso said that. My father collected some of his smaller works. All taken, *phhft*." She expelled air from her mouth. "A nasty little man, that Picasso, but I agree." Her tone dismissive. "So does Irati. It's those protests she attends."

Alert, Aimée leaned forward. A new angle to consider. "Protests? Irati doesn't strike me as political."

"*Phfft!* The young these days," Madame said, as if that explained it. "We met at the poll during the last election. We both voted Socialist. Irati joked that we're the only two Socialists in the *quartier*. Our mayor's a Taittinger, the Champagne seigneur; we're his fiefdom." Madame de Boucher's chignon loosened as she nodded. A strand of white hair fell, softening the contours of her thin face. "*C'est tout*. Then I get this! A mistake. No interest to me."

Aimée sat up.

"May I see?"

Madame de Boucher used an aluminum rod with pincers at the end to clutch some papers on the divan.

Aimée took the white paper, folded pamphlet-style, titled *Euskadi Action*. The Basque-language leaflet didn't make sense to her either. But an address on rue Duban and the date Sunday at 6:30 P.M., that much she understood. The rest she'd find out.

Madame de Boucher nodded, staring at the *gâteau* Basque. "Aren't you going to cut me a slice?"

*  *  *

"CRIME IN OUR *quartier?*" Dubouchet, the on-duty sergeant in the Passy Commissariat, grinned, showing yellowed teeth. "Just the usual: rich teenagers thrill-shoplifting, *domestiques* stealing from their employer. What goes around comes around, eh?"

She'd come to check with Thesset about the Mercedes, but he'd gone off duty. "But on the *télé*, the news announced this crime of passion. . . ."

"I can't talk about ongoing investigations, Mademoiselle." Dubouchet's voice turned serious.

Great: now he'd clammed up. And Thesset, her source, was gone. The smell of hot printer toner wafted from behind her. An old-fashioned heater rumbled, sending out dribbles of heat.

"*Zut!*" Gandon, a middle-aged lieutenant sitting at a desk, ground out his cigarette in his demitasse saucer. "Dubouchet forgets the glory days, our unrivaled crimes." He opened a drawer, pulled out a thick stapled manuscript with relish. "Bit of a history buff myself. My little opus, which I hope to publish next year, could enlighten you."

"Might want to finish writing the thing first, Gandon," Dubouchet said in a tired voice.

"Mademoiselle, our arrondissement encompasses two zip codes, with a Taittinger as reigning mayor. Despite our current *haut bourgeois* reputation, I recount our long history. It's fascinating reading." Gandon thumbed the pages, warming to his subject. "Eighteen seventy, the anti-Bonapartist Victor Noir's assassination by Napoleon III's nephew. A Républican hero. Legend goes women visit his tomb for fertility; go figure, but it adds glamour, eh, a footnote to history." Gandon winked.

She shifted her feet, hoping this would lead somewhere.

"The attempt on Clemenceau's life, 1919," he said. "I'll have you know we've even had our own serial killer, Dr. Marcel Petiot, a charmer who dismembered his patients, hid the bits in the courtyard well, then, copying his heroes the *boches*, incinerated them in his homemade crematorium. Of course, the real 'French Connection' heroin king, André Condemine, was gunned down not ten blocks from here."

Gandon's face was suffused with pride. Aimée unwound her silk scarf, wishing for an open window to ventilate the tepid, stale air.

"Who would have thought?" She hadn't bargained on an earful. But the eager Gandon knew his turf. "Anything interesting on the political front?"

"*Bien sûr*, we've had our share." Gandon thumbed the pages. "The 1980 synagogue bombing on rue Copernic, terrible. Four dead. I carried out what was left of the bodies." He shook his head. "We had political terrorists—Action Directe, who'd hooked up with Carlos the Jackal. Not to mention a cannibal." He looked up for Aimée's admiration. "Name me another *quartier* that had a Japanese student cut up his teacher and eat her, eh?"

Aimée tried to look impressed.

"Even René Bousquet couldn't hide his Vichy past. It caught up with him right in his doorway on Avenue Raphaël. Not two months ago, Princess Di departed on our patch too . . . don't forget that."

"But Morbier's in custody," she said. "You're the only one who can help."

For the first time, Léo looked up with interest.

"So don't do this for *me*, do it for *him*. Please, you've known Morbier for years, *n'est-ce pas?*"

Léo put on the headphones. Sighed. "What do you want this time?"

Aimée wanted to hug her. But Léo wouldn't like that. Instead, she grabbed a pencil and the graph paper notepad on Léo's desk.

"Do that triangulation voodoo you do so well. Record the calls, pinpoint the cell phone location."

"National security involved?"

The lead pencil tip snapped. What if Léo had just hit it on the head? Militant French Basques? She'd think about that later. "Morbier's girlfriend was strangled. I found her. But someone else was in the house. Her daughter blames Morbier, but she's misguided."

"Misguided?"

But it felt more complicated that that.

"Either mistaken and looking for an easy answer or . . ." She hesitated. ". . . lying. I don't know."

"Never boring with you, Aimée." Léo typed in Irati's phone number. "Any idea of the transmission area?"

"In Passy, the 16th." Aimée pointed to the map covering the wall divided into arrondissements. "I figure the murderer will contact her."

"Doesn't sound like Morbier's type at all."

"She was Basque. I don't have anything else to go on."

"You think the murderer would call her daughter? Make a

demand, more like it." Léo swiveled her chair and put on the reading glasses hanging from her neck.

"That's what I need to find out." Aimée winced. "Her daughter's not too happy with me right now."

"Doesn't do to piss people like that off. But then tact's not your strong suit." Léo sucked in her breath. Shook her head.

Aimée shivered in the barely heated apartment.

She leaned on Léo's desk. "If I don't find the murderer, the evidence points to Morbier. It smells, Léo."

Léo paused. "And of course you don't want the *flics* involved."

"You got it, Léo." Aimée swallowed. "Blinded by love, Morbier wanted me to protect Xavierre. And I didn't."

Léo shook her head. "I'll input the phone's ESN and MIN code. When a call's made or received, my scanner will pick it up. Remember, the longer the call, the better the trace. For me to locate the phone, it needs to emit the roaming signal so the next nearby antenna tower picks it up. It's all about the towers."

"Don't all cell phones now do that continuously?"

"Not yet, but Big Brother's coming. Right now that feature's a military tool." Léo looked up. "Tracking depends on the signal strength of the antenna masts. This wind doesn't help. It scatters the electromagnetic waves like confetti. Say your prayers that the radio transmitter tower out there cooperates."

"Only one way to find out." Aimée dug her cell phone from her pocket and punched in the number.

Irati's number flashed on the screen. The halogen light cast a bluish glare on the window.

"*Oui,*" Irati answered on the first ring. A breathy quality, as if she'd run to the phone.

"Any word, Irati?"

Pause. Glass clinked in the background. "Word?"

"On your mother's funeral? It's Aimée."

Disappointment and something else tinged her voice. "I told you—"

"I'm sorry for this afternoon," Aimée interrupted.

A click on Aimée's cell phone indicated another call. She ignored it.

Léo rolled one hand in a circular motion, mouthed, "Keep her on."

"Please listen: I want to help you," she said. "Do you understand, Irati?"

"L . . . leave me alone." Short shallow breaths.

But she hadn't hung up.

"*Enfin*, I lost my father in a bomb explosion. But the *flics* closed the file; the Ministry ignored my requests." That yawning hole inside opened, that need to know why, if it was a terrorist, an informer, a mistake. "I know the feeling. Afraid, alone. . . ."

A sob came over the line.

"Irati, you can talk to me," she said. "Whatever happened, I won't judge you. If you're in danger, you have my word, no *flics* involved."

Léo mouthed, "*Got* it."

"You haven't gone to the *flics* again, have you?" Irati's voice was a whisper.

A cold feeling hit the pit of Aimée's stomach. Why did Irati want to know? Léo pointed to the address that had popped up on her screen. 40 rue Raynouard. At least that proved that it worked and the towers in the area were functioning.

"Stay away, not safe to. . . ." Irati trailed off.

A creaking noise like a door opening, footsteps.

The phone buzzed. Dead.

The address disappeared from the screen.

"*Zut!* At least we established the trace. But it's more important to find out who calls her and their location. Not all that different, right?"

"In theory, if the call's active long enough, the towers cooperate, and her caller's not in a dead zone. But I'd need my second scanner free and operational to nail it. Takes two to tango." Léo gave her a pointed look. "Your five minutes are up."

Aimée lingered, pulling her scarf tighter against the draft. "Let's say her caller was in close range, nearby, in the *quartier*?"

"That's a best-case scenario," Léo said. "Otherwise, compare it to the chances of finding a brown lentil in that." Léo jerked her thumb toward a 25-kilo sack of green lentils.

In the meantime, so much could go wrong.

A velvet-like fur brushed her leg. She looked down to see a svelte Siamese cat, turquoise-eyed, yawn, then stretch.

"Meet Marconi," Léo said. "He's hungry. His pâté's on the counter."

No proletarian, this cat. He ate better than Léo. But Aimée kept that observation to herself as she spooned the glistening pâté into a ceramic bowl glazed with the words CHAT LUNATIQUE.

Léo motioned from her wheelchair. "Irati's got a call."

Aimée rushed to see Irati's number on the screen. Her pulse raced. She glanced at the clock. "Can you pinpoint the location of who's calling her, their number?"

"Try patience, Aimée, and hope she stays on the line so I can track it."

Crackling noises. Beeping, a muffled voice: ". . . a package. Got that?"

Irati's number disappeared again from the screen.

"What's wrong?"

"I'd say Irati's cell phone ran out of battery."

*Merde.*

Disappointed, she stared at the screen. "But you'll contact me if there's another call, right?"

A hooded look veiled Léo's face. "I shouldn't, but . . . seems like you and Morbier need all the help you can get."

On her way to the door, Aimée saw the soft curved mound, the cat's indentations on the duvet of Léo's hospital bed. At least Léo didn't sleep alone any more.

"*Merci*, Léo."

"Don't thank me yet," Léo said.

\* \* \*

ON RUE DU Louvre, Aimée handed the change back to the taxi driver. "Keep it." Her investment for rainy-night taxi karma.

"*Merci*, Mademoiselle."

The streetlight glowed yellow above the wet pavement. Quiet hovered for a brief moment as traffic paused at the rue de Rivoli intersection. The Louvre's lit limestone façade glowed like a misted pearl. Saddened, she thought of this spot last night when she'd met Morbier. His anguish, the slight tremor in his hand. Why hadn't she insisted he tell her more?

She tried to brush the guilt aside. Guilt, a luxury she didn't have time for. Plus it got her nowhere. Her phone beeped with a saved message. Thesset with news on the Mercedes?

She hit PLAY. Melac's voice: "Delayed. Don't wait for me."

Great! A bottle of Veuve Clicquot setting her back part of a paycheck, a cold office with a pile of work. No doubt with his career to consider, Melac had rethought testing the waters. She couldn't blame him. So he'd deserted Morbier too.

It was useless to go home; she knew she wouldn't be able to sleep. Might as well work. The wire cage elevator, circa 1910, shuddered up to the second floor. Stopped and refused to budge.

Par for the evening, she thought, opening the accordion metal doors and trudging up the next flight.

She unlocked Leduc Detective's frosted glass door, hung her coat up on the hook, and wedged several juniper logs in the grate. She blew until the coals burst into flame, pulled the mohair throw around her for warmth, and sat cross-legged on the floor.

The fax paper on the wood-paneled wall stared back at her.

Useless to try to work, too.

She heard the key turning in the lock. The door opened to a gust of cold air. For a moment, her hand trembled.

"Communing with the fire spirits, Aimée?" René asked, unwrapping his muffler. "Or sacrificing more logs to appease the god of fire?"

She turned to look at René, then back at the names on the paper flickering in the firelight.

"I think you've got something, René."

"I do?" He set down his cane, unzipped his judo bag, and took out a bottle of Evian. "Nice and toasty in here." He scanned the files on his desk, blinked in surprise. "All caught up too. A first. You even finished my proposals. *Merci.*"

"Not quite. Another pile to tackle." She pushed the mohair throw aside, picked up a marker. "But you might have hit the right nail. Maybe even on the right head. Gives me a scenario to work with."

"Care to explain? With a nice Veuve Clicquot getting warm?"

She'd forgotten. No reason to burden René, as usual, with her nonexistent love life. She wanted to pick his brain.

"Always good to have a spare bottle. On sale, too." Opening the double window, she breathed in the frigid air and stuck the bottle behind the window box of red geraniums. "Natural cooling."

She shut the window, latched it.

"Mind if I bounce an idea off you?"

"Now?" René glanced at the time. "Five minutes' worth."

She took the blue feather duster from the cupboard, pointed the tip at her map. "Say the wounded killer comes to Xavierre's for help." She pointed to the taped gravel, which she'd colored with red marker to indicate blood. "Bleeding, he leaves traces. After he gains entry to the rear bedroom, Xavierre tries to put him off: her guests, the party, she explains. Morbier, jealous, watches from the garden, leaving footprints, and loses his tiepin. He sees them argue."

"And you know this for a fact?" René sat back in his orthopedic chair.

She shrugged. "Morbier left his tiepin and his footprints."

"Quite an impressive state-of-the-art crime-scene reconstruction," he said.

"Homemade does the job," she said. "Just listen, René; see if it makes sense. Guests pull up, Morbier leaves. At the party, Xavierre pleads illness, some excuse. After a quick Champagne toast, Irati shoos the guests out. Meanwhile we show up, the old couple leaves. Remember?"

"The complaining geriatrics?" he said. "What about the caterers' noises in the kitchen?"

"We saw no van or truck, right?" she said. "What if those

noises were coming from the impatient killer? Say they were, and we complicated matters, messing up his agenda. Xavierre needs us to leave."

"Why?" René said. "It would make more sense that she'd want us to stay, if she's in danger."

Aimée pointed the feather duster to the salon. "True. Let's say that at that juncture, she counted on being able to handle him. Using leverage, I don't know." Then she pointed to the rear bedroom. "But the argument escalates—say he demands that Xavierre find a doctor or let him stay. She refuses, threatens to expose him. She runs out the rear terrace doors; but, desperate, he catches her, strangles her." She jabbed the paper. "He has to prevent her from turning him in." Pointed to the Mercedes photo. "The killer hears you close the gate, assumes we've left. He runs back to her car, drives away. We know the rest."

"So if Irati confirms this, they'll release Morbier?"

"That's the point. Morbier's the main suspect in a crime of passion, as the news termed it. Why?"

René shook his head. "But you're going to tell me, right?"

"If you were Irati, with your mother murdered almost before your eyes, would it make sense for you to lie? To corroborate Morbier's guilt?"

"You're going somewhere with this, right?" René stretched his short legs. Checked his watch.

Cool your handmade shoes, she wanted to say.

"Say this killer calls Irati, threatens that the same thing will happen to her if she exposes him to the *flics*," she said. "Irati's hysterical: her mother's been murdered; she's threatened."

"A few issues you've neglected," René said. "The fiancé, this Robbé; the possibility that the killer was a guest who left and returned to meet Xavierre outside and then killed her."

Shadows flickered on the office walls.

"That could work. Still, it doesn't explain the kitchen noises, or why a wounded killer, who was bleeding outside, would attend the party. But Robbé's scared. Irati was calling the shots when I tried to talk to them. Both were eager to see the back of me."

"So the killer threatens Irati with her fiancé's death unless she cooperates," said René, nodding. "That might make me lie, to save the person I loved."

"*Exactement.*" Aimée knelt down, adding a log to the now-sputtering fire. "Didn't you ask me if I was 'appeasing the fire god'? It fits, in a way. But you'll never appease your mother's murderer. Tonight Irati asked if I'd gone to the *flics* again, then said 'Stay away . . . not safe' before someone walked in the room and she hung up."

"But you're neglecting a simple scenario." René tented his fingers, interested now. "One you won't like. Say this blood has nothing to do with the killer or Xavierre. What if it's dog's blood?"

"Good point. But the lab results—"

"Will confirm or deny it," René interrupted. "So for argument's sake, say the blood has no bearing. The old couple borrowed the Mercedes, they're unfamiliar with the car so it takes them time to start it. Say Morbier, who'd asked for your help, has second thoughts en route to Lyon. Feels foolish, jealous, whatever. He instructs his driver to turn back. Or dismisses him. Either way, say Morbier returns, sees us inside, and is afraid Xavierre's revealing why she avoided his phone calls: she wants to break it off. She doesn't, of course, but what if she was afraid? But Morbier doesn't know that. He waits, lures her onto the terrace, accuses her . . . then. . . ."

Aimée dropped the duster, battling a seed of doubt. "How could you think Morbier . . . ?" Her throat caught.

"Not me." René's brow creased. "But I'm saying that's ten to one how the *flics* would look at this. His driver's his alibi. So why hasn't Morbier been released?"

She sank on the recamier. "I asked him that."

"Didn't answer, did he?" René averted his eye. "The facts don't look good. I'm sorry, Aimée."

"Morbier's no amateur. He knows the system. It doesn't make sense." She stared at René. "Unless. . . ."

"Give up, Aimée."

"The mustard stains on his suit."

"Eh?" René's eyes widened. "So he's hungry, stops at a *routier*. *Non*, not many of them any more. So a rest stop where the food's in plastic. He changes his mind and heads back to Paris."

"The first part's brilliant, René."

"All this from a mustard stain?" René shook his head.

She remembered Morbier pacing on the wet pavement, the thrumming of the waiting car's engine, his black wool coat glistening with mist, open to his corduroy jacket.

"If anything, the timing could confirm his guilt," said René, his voice terse. "Look. Morbier's my friend too. This hurts. It's terrible. But right now, leave it alone. Don't pursue what guarantees his—"

"Innocence?" She picked up her cell phone, scrolled down her address list. Hit a number. "Inés? *Oui, ça va? Non*, I'm fine. Silly question, but does Emile still run Les Acacias? Retired? Of course . . . your son? Nice to keep it in the family. My number's the same, I'd appreciate if he could call me. You too."

She hung up. Rubbed her hands in front of the fire. Warmth crept up her arms.

"Why didn't I think of it?" She shook her head. "Emile's son runs the *routier* now, still a trucker stop with the best *frites* and *saucisson* on the A6 approach to Cachan."

"The A6 south to Lyon?"

"My father met his suburban *indicateurs* at Emile's. A lot of the *flics* did. The old-fashioned *routier*, good food, easy to blend in, and everyone's on their way somewhere. A quick getaway."

"Meaning?"

"Let's say Morbier met an *indicateur* there to get information on Lyon," she said. "He loves Emile's *saucisson* smothered in *moutarde de* Dijon."

"You're serious?" René's brow creased in thought. "But then why not. . . ."

"Reveal his informer?" She shook her head. "He'd never get another whisper."

How many times had she seen her father unearthing a lead, checking every detail cobble by painstaking cobble, finding it a dead end? Then came the one odd piece at the back of the file or discrepancy glossed over—or rechecked for the fourth time— that broke the case.

"Sounds far-fetched to me," said René. "You're reaching, Aimée."

"You'd drop your socks if you realized how much a *flic*'s work owes to an informer's tip," she said. "Like a slow-moving train gathering information—a name, the girlfriend's last address, bits and pieces that add up."

"Protecting a source, fair enough. But that goes both ways," René said.

"Depends on how deep the source goes, his cover, the connections, a lot of intangibles. Half of the *flic*'s work's done by listening to snitches; the other half, methodical plodding."

The reasons she hated criminal investigation.

"*Et alors*, say that's so, say the informer's related to Morbier's investigation in Lyon." René stood, did a neck roll. "My turn." He took the black marker, reached on his tiptoes, and circled Xavierre's name.

"What do you really know about her?"

Good question. Morbier had revealed little about his relationship until last night.

"Not much more than you," she said. "I'd only met her on the street once before. But she was in love."

René drew a column. "In love. *Voilà*, we also know she was *haute bourgeoise*, moneyed, lived in a chic *quartier*; she'd rekindled an old affair with Morbier—"

"But why her?" Aimée interrupted. "Why now, with her daughter's wedding, guests, the preparations?"

"Let me finish." He pointed the duster handle like a school-teacher. "Very important. We know she's Basque."

"True. Yet Xavierre and Irati don't fit the Basque Separatist profile in the headlines—hiding revolutionaries in safe houses after armed attacks and bombings."

She'd gotten nowhere with Agustino about Xavierre's past. But he had been hiding something. Cybèle had denied her sister's links with ETA. But Aimée wondered if Xavierre had supported the cause in other ways.

If it smelled, her father always said, track it down. Or it would bite your sinuses like ripe Port Salut.

Before she could pursue it, René's cell phone trilled on his desk. He glanced at the number, then reached for his judo bag.

"*Cherie?* Ready?"

Aimée looked up in surprise to see a wide smile on his face. He clicked off his phone and headed to the door.

"Hot date?"

"If that's what you call pot stickers with her parents at Chez Chun."

"The woman from the dojo? I call it progress." Aimée said. "Chinatown's perfect on a night like this."

She felt happy for René. It was time he met someone and it worked out.

He shook his head. "A Marais hole in the wall run by her uncle, near her family's wholesale luggage shop. Traditional types who think I should learn their Wenzhou dialect."

Aimée grinned. "And you're still here?"

He paused at the door. "What about you?"

She bit back her frustration, seeing the names on the wall, the looming long evening alone. Stood and booted up her computer. "Work to catch up on."

He hesitated. His phone trilled again.

"Try and get her alone next time, René."

* * *

IN THE WC down the hall, Aimée splashed cold water on her face and leaned on the cracked porcelain sink. In the soap-speckled mirror, she studied a fine line under her eye. Expression lines, my foot, she thought. She squeezed the tube of Dior concealer. Empty. Like the evening ahead.

Emptier for Morbier in a cell. And a pity party would get her nowhere. She had work to do.

Back in Leduc Detective, she blew on the fire and sipped her espresso. Cold.

Until she discovered more about Xavierre, she was spinning her wheels. She had no suspects to point away from Morbier.

She needed to know this woman: her family, her past, her secrets.

Everyone left traces; the hard part was finding the significant ones. Start with basics, what she knew. Xavierre's state-of-the-art kitchen would have required building permits.

Online, she entered the Ville de Paris Web site, searched *La Direction de l'aménagement urbain et de la construction*, and input Xavierre's address. The notation indicated the contractor's name, license, and renovation work totaling a year. All a matter of public record. A hefty sum for work that she figured should have taken four months at most. From there she dug deeper, from the city's approval to the renovation contract.

The approval form listed the owner as Xavierre D'Eslay *née* Contrexo. One bright star shone in the evening: now she had Xavierre's maiden name. Her tracking possibilities widened.

Morbier had met Xavierre Contrexo more than twenty years ago. At that time, post-Sorbonne riots, he'd been patrolling with Aimée's father on the beat. If Xavierre had been a student in Bayonne, had Morbier met her on holiday in the Basque country? According to Cybèle, her family herded sheep.

Or had he and Xavierre met in Paris, at a student demonstration? She let that simmer, sat back—and found it staring her right in the face: ask Cybèle. She tried immediately. No answer on her cell phone. She tried the house. No answer.

Determined now, she thought of the next family member, Cybèle's ill husband in Bayonne. A minute later, directory assistance connected her.

A gruff voice. "*Allô?*"

"Monsieur Urioste?"

"Who's this, at this time of night?"

Nine P.M.? "*Excusez-moi*, Monsieur, but I'm calling from Paris regarding the investigation. . . ."

"You a journalist?" he said. "Call in the morning."

He'd given her the perfect opportunity. "Before the rumors reach epic proportions, we at *Le Parisien* wanted to confirm—"

"Rumors? You're all snakes." Pause. "What rumors?"

"Xavierre d'Eslay's link with the Basque ETA."

Instead of hearing the phone slammed down, she heard a clearing of his throat. "That old story?" A snort. "Happened years ago. My sister-in-law married money, didn't know us after that, changed her tune, believe me."

A dry laugh. She sensed he didn't hold warm feelings for his sister-in-law.

"I need more than that, Monsieur, for my article," she said. "That's if you want the *facts* presented, not distortions."

"Check with your kind, those rodents over at *Sud Ouest*." *Sud Ouest* was the Bordeaux daily newspaper. "Talk to the archives and for once get your facts straight. And don't quote me." He hung up.

The *Sud Ouest* archives in Bordeaux didn't answer. But Martine, her best friend since the lycée and a journalist, could help.

"Aimée . . . hold on a moment," said Martine.

Singing, music, and laughter sounded loudly in the background. Martine lived with Gilles and his children in a huge flat overlooking the Bois de Boulogne. "Karaoke night for sixteen-year-olds," Martine shouted. "Like the old days, remember?"

"I'd like to forget them, Martine."

She heard a door shut, the flick of a lighter, a sharp inhalation. Martine smoked a pack a day. Aimée reached in her desk drawer for the strip of "stop smoking" patches. Empty.

"Now I can talk," Martine said. "*Ça va?*" Martine took another drag, not waiting for an answer. "*Bon,* I shouldn't say it but I'll say it anyway. A Tuesday night, and you're working late? You need a man."

Not this again.

Martine made it her perpetual mission to set Aimée up. Blind dates, dinner parties, discreet introductions at wine bar openings—all disasters.

"Buff. Strong, of course," Martine said. "I'm thinking of Gilles's friend, career Navy and a champion diver, who commands the Naval underwater recovery unit in Toulon."

She meant GIGN, the military elite assault unit.

"Don't you have a weakness for men in Speedos?" Martine continued.

Speedos were one thing, career Navy another.

"Get back on shore, Martine," she said. "Do me a huge favor: tap into the vein at *Sud Ouest* archives for Xavierre d'Eslay *née* Contrexo, links to ETA."

Martine, a journalist, maintained an extensive network of contacts. *De rigueur* in her job.

"Now? But I'm jammed with my Radio France deadline, Aimée. Our four-part agribusiness program airs tomorrow."

"Can't the farmers wait an hour, Martine? They've waited this long."

"ETA's old news. *Passé.*" She exhaled. "No one's interested in explosions in vacant police stations or post offices. There's a cease-fire in the offing that they voted for in a referendum."

"But what if this bears somehow on the *haute bourgeoise* matron's murder—"

"The one on the *télé,* here in the 16th?" Martine coughed. "Near us?"

"*Et voilà*," Aimée said.

"See, we have a dark side. Haven't I likened our *quartier* to an elegant older aunt with a surprisingly hip and edgy side?"

Martine only lived there because Gilles had inherited a large flat in the building, comprising the whole floor. Fourteen-plus rooms overlooking the Bois de Boulogne.

"Think of your article explored from the angle of her past links to ETA," Aimée said, "her relationship with a Commissaire Divisionnaire, highlighting the skewed investigation based on circumstantial evidence?"

"Why do I feel . . . ? Wait, Morbier's new squeeze. That's her?"

"Was. Your nose should be twitching like a fox at the hunt, Martine."

A long inhale.

"Except that Morbier's investigating and doing his job, Aimée. What's it to you?"

"*Au contraire*: he's the *suspect*."

"*Quoi!* I don't believe it."

"Believe this." Aimée drained the demitasse of cold espresso and told her. "I need anything you can find."

"Let's see," Martine said. "One of the Radio France producers has a brother working at *Sud Ouest*. Used to. How far back?"

"Say twenty-five years," Aimée said. "And dig into the new generation of Basques," she said, trying to make her understand. "Euskadi Action demonstrations. The daughter's on their mailing list; she's afraid, too."

"Intriguing, Aimée." Pause. "But you'll join us for Gilles's birthday Sunday? An intimate dinner, close friends. Promise?"

Aimée groaned inside. Of course Martine needed another woman at the table—a date—for Gilles's naval commander diver. She hated to think of the long evening of underwater exploits.

"Gilles loves Veuve Clicquot, like you."

At least she had that covered. "You'll let me know what you hear, Martine?"

"Make that two bottles, Aimée." Martine hung up.

All this had taken time. She had an idea. It would cost her, and yet. . . . She sighed and grabbed a padded envelope. From René's drawer she chose a cell phone from their collection, checked the battery, and locked the office door.

\* \* \*

SHE LEFT HER scooter and, still in high-tops, walked past the verdigris iron Métro entrance at Louvre-Rivoli. She needed to walk, to think, to contact Morbier. And she hoped her little plan would work.

She followed the dimly lit quai, pulling her faux fur tighter. Under the cloud-filled night sky, she crossed Pont Neuf, the misted Seine gurgling below, and walked into shadowed Place Dauphine.

Ghosts everywhere, she thought, whispering in the wind, funneling past the damp corners, the skeletal trees, the seventeenth-century lawyers' quarters—long a bistro—that she'd frequented with Morbier.

Beyond lay the Tribunal, massive columns lost in shadow. A squirrel skittered over the gravel and disappeared behind a slatted bench. Otherwise, the triangular square lay deserted across from the lighted bistro. Her hopes rose after she turned onto quai de l'Horloge near the jail door. The same *flic* from this afternoon stood at his guard post. With luck, he'd remember her.

Better yet, allow her into the visiting area.

He guarded the Gothic thick-planked door dotted with square nail heads, leading to *le dépôt*, the jail under La Conciergerie, originally Jean the Good's medieval kitchen, often mistaken by tourists for the museum entrance to Marie Antoinette's cell.

"Long shift, eh?" She flashed a smile and her pass. "I'm back again. Anyone released from the *garde à vue* this afternoon?"

"Not through here." He stifled a yawn. "Visiting closed hours ago, too. Check with the bureau in the courtyard at eight A.M."

Her heart fell. Poor Morbier. And in this cold.

Time for her plan. She pulled out her checkbook, tore off a deposit slip, wrote MORBIER URGENT, and taped it to the padded envelope with the cell phone.

"Papers came from the lawyer." She smiled. "It would save me a trip tomorrow if you could leave this for Morbier with the duty sergeant." She racked her brain for his name. At one time she'd known most of them. During her childhood, half the force had played Friday-night poker at her kitchen table. "Sergeant Roche, that's the one. He knows me." She widened her smile. Debated a come-hither look.

"Never hurts to ask, Mademoiselle." He winked, then nodded to an arriving *flic*. "But I'm off duty."

She edged closer as he took out his keys. "But since you'll pass by Roche's desk . . . it would mean so much."

He hesitated.

"Look, Morbier's my godfather."

A hand shot out and he slipped the envelope into his pocket before the *flic* could see it.

\* \* \*

"FLIRTING WITH FLICS? Nice, and after your little sermon."

The hair rose on the back of her neck. She spun around to see Melac, his face just this side of craggy, defined by pale gray eyes with an unnerving focus. Arms crossed, he stood under the Resistance Memorial plaque on the Préfecture's wall.

"No law against that," she said.

The streetlight caught the pockmarks from bullet holes left by the Germans in 1944, the fresh flower remembrance for the fallen, and Melac's silver belt buckle.

"I remember you said that—before you broke a few last month," Melac said.

She felt his piercing vision going through her.

"All water under the bridge now." She pointed to the sluggish black water of the Seine. "But you canceled tonight, and now you're spying on me?"

"With this?" He lifted a gym bag. "Things got complicated upstairs."

"Most things do."

He stepped closer. A day's stubble shaded his chin. He wore black jeans, a black leather jacket, and a thick-ribbed blue wool scarf knotted at his neck.

"What's that saying? Don't give excuses, just apologize later?"

She hadn't remembered his eyes. How big they were. Why did she feel twinges of guilt?

"Nice, Melac." She pointed to the pink hearts trimming his scarf's edge. "Your new look? Or from an admirer?"

"My daughter knitted this," he said. "Now she won't stop. I've got one in every color."

Aimée grinned.

And then he pulled her close in his warmth, his citrus scent. His lambskin leather jacket brushed her cheek.

"Look, Melac, I understand, ethics, compromising your work. It's not fair. . . ."

"I've missed you too, Aimée." He lifted her chin. His fingers traced her cheekbone. His warm fingers. Tiny beads of moisture clung to the black hair curling over his neck.

"What plan are you hatching in that mind of yours?" he said.

As if she'd tell him. He couldn't or wouldn't help. "I don't get it, Melac. Morbier's a respected Commissaire Divisionnaire, held on circumstantial evidence—as you pointed out—but you act like I'm subversive."

"Sabotaging Morbier's chances would be more accurate," he said, his finger resting on her cheekbone. "Politics are playing out behind the scenes. Don't you know that by now?"

"Morbier's navigated the waters and survived this long. He's risen to the top," she said. And then it clicked: the fall guy.

Was that it? A shiver trailed her spine.

"You're saying it's too late?"

"I don't know," Melac said. "No one's talking upstairs. I tried. Everyone needs protection these days. Sometimes from themselves."

Was Melac holding something back? She'd get more if she listened and appeared to acquiesce.

Morbier's twenty-four hours in the *garde à vue* should end in the morning, barring discovery of concrete evidence of his guilt. She prayed Roche, the duty sergeant, would pass the cell phone to Morbier. She had to talk with him.

Melac drew a breath.

"But questions have been raised," he said. "There's an RG file. Not a place you should nose around in right now."

"An RG file exists?"

"The victim's got a dossier."

If Xavierre had a file from Renseignements Généraux, which handled threats to internal security, it meant one thing: ETA. The RG had prioritized ETA and their activities from the seventies to the early nineties, when a special military police unit had been formed to cover the Basque region.

Did hope exist for Morbier after all? But she kept these thoughts to herself.

"At least you tried. *Merci.*"

"They're stretched to the limit with events in Lyon, the *flic* killer in the *Imprimerie Nationale* heist," he said, rubbing his forehead. "Plus the continuing priority hunt for the phantom Fiat Uno speeding away from Princess Diana's crash. An ongoing headache."

A white-and-blue police car sped by, lights flashing, bathing the buildings and Melac's face in blue. Brakes squealed as it turned, bumping over the cobbles into the yawning entrance of the Préfecture.

"On top of that, my leave's canceled," he said. "Now I turn around, head back to Brittany, and explain to my daughter. Effective tomorrow night, I'm back at my desk."

He gave a little smile. "But we could have that drink. My train's later."

"*C'est dommage*, a shame the Champagne's chilling outside with the geraniums."

He gave a knowing nod. "Done that myself." He put his arm

around her. "But the bar on Île Saint-Louis serves a decent *coupe* of Taittinger."

Chez Georges, around the corner from her place.

"Just one, Melac," she said. "That's all."

*Wednesday Morning*

THROUGH A HAZE of sleep, Aimée heard beeping from the hallway. Struggling awake, she found her legs entangled by sheets, an arm around her shoulder. Soft warm breaths on her neck. The pale apricot rays of dawn wavered over the discarded clothes on the wood floor. And she remembered. Melac.

Her cell phone rang again. Miles Davis stirred on the floor, blinked his black eyes. Closed them.

She slipped from Melac's arms, grabbing her father's old flannel robe. She shivered at the cold floor. Good god, where had she left her phone? She found it at the bottom of her bag hanging from the coat hook.

A number she didn't recognize. Her feet were freezing on the creaking cold wood.

"*Oui?*"

"What's the emergency, Leduc?" Morbier's disjointed voice was broken up by static.

"Morbier, are you all right?" she asked. Her knuckles clenching the phone whitened.

The flush of a toilet. "I've been better. Make it quick, Leduc."

"The RG have a file on Xavierre."

"That's it? But there's a file on everybody," he said, irritated. "Thick as phone books."

"Everybody was in ETA? How was she involved? How did you meet her?"

Pause. "I'm an old fool." She heard the catch in his throat. "No one ever came close to her, Leduc."

"I understand. But tell me, Morbier."

Shouts and clanging metal. "We met at a demonstration in the early seventies near the Champs-Elysées, typical pot-au-feu, troublemakers, students. She was part of a trio from Bayonne, just students. . . ." His voice faded.

She thought of Irati's involvement with Euskadi Action: like mother, like daughter?

"En route to Lyon, you stopped at Emile's *routier*, right? That's your alibi?"

"Don't go there, Leduc," he said, anger vibrating in the static.

"But your driver. . . ."

Coughing. "Told him to go home. You know the rules of the *routier*. Solo."

Bad to worse. The informer his only alibi. She thought fast. "But couldn't Melac talk to your informer on the quiet?"

"*Merde!*" She heard the gush of water, a squeaking, like a faucet turned off. "Leave it alone."

"Why?"

"Listen," he said.

She heard dripping water.

"*Compris*, Leduc?"

"A leaky faucet," she said, exasperated. "Give me something to work with, Morbier. Anything."

"I did." Pause. "Think."

Her shoulders tensed. "A leak. You're investigating a leak. . . ."

"Trust no one, Leduc. No one."

The phone went dead. The floor creaked behind her and she jumped.

"Who's that, so early?" Melac said, his warm arms encircling her waist.

"The plumber." She said the first thing that came into her head and shoved the phone into her robe pocket. "He wants to finish work on our floor. At this hour, too!"

He pulled her closer, nuzzled her neck. "But you're shaking. Your hand's like ice."

*Trust no one*, Morbier said.

"Poor circulation." She managed a smile, steeled herself not to pull away. "Coffee before your train?"

His eyebrow lifted. "That call shook you up, I can tell."

And I can't trust you, she thought, even after last night. Had he overheard her talking on the phone?

She exhaled, shrugged. Miles Davis whined at the door. "Our concierge neglects things. It's not the first time." She made a fist and cocked it to indicate drinking. "The woman's got a vendetta against me, leaves messages. . . ."

"But I can block those calls, if the number. . . ."

Why had he turned so curious? She needed to quit rambling, quit these lies before she messed up. She needed him out of here.

She nestled under his shoulder, steered him toward the kitchen. "How about *un express* before Miles Davis waters the trees and I walk you to the Métro?"

\* \* \*

Aimée parked her scooter in the viaduct under the elevated Métro at Passy. Light drizzle beaded the curling white bark of the birch trees, and her eyelashes. She wished she'd worn rain gear instead of a leather coat over her ruffled silk blouse and black denim pencil skirt.

She found the café nestled at the bottom of the steps. At the crowded café counter, she wedged in the back among the horserace bettors. Wisps of blue smoke spiraled to the nicotine-stained ceiling. She almost didn't hear her phone ring amid the whooshing of the milk steamer.

"Aimée?" Martine's voice whipped in the wind. "Where are you?"

Aimée peered over the shoulder of the man shouting at the horses on the *télé* mounted in the wall. "In the back."

Martine waved from the window.

"*Voilà*, I see you now."

A man slapped his PMU—*Pari Mutuel Urbain*, the racing association betting slip—on the counter. He shouldered his way through the three-deep crowd toward the cashier. The fetid air resulting from too many bodies, wet wool, and smoke filled the café.

"Trying your luck on the horses, Aimée?" Martine said, raising her voice over the din of the *télé* and the shouts of the patrons. "Nice and quiet, too."

"*Désolée*, the only place I remembered near Radio France."

Martine smiled at the bearded man behind the counter and ordered. "*Un thé à la menthe.*"

"You found something, Martine?" Aimée set down her espresso.

"Yes and no."

Hope pounded in Aimée's chest.

Martine dipped the tea bag in the steaming cup of water. "Don't get me started, Aimée."

Startled, she looked sideways at Martine. "What's that look on your face mean?"

"It's not good."

"The Basques?"

Martine opened a pack of Muratti Ambassadors, tapped a filter on the zinc countertop, and flicked her orange lighter. She blew a stream of smoke over her shoulder. "Did I tell you about the hoopla? A madhouse at Radio France." Martine made a moue of distaste. "They cut my agribusiness feature in half. Assigned me to cover tonight's Basque referendum reception, minor royalty—a Spanish princess—in attendance. To highlight the historical and cultural implications of 'new' Franco-Spanish relations. Boring. We're becoming as royalty-mad as the BBC."

Aimée leaned her arms on the counter. "I'm more interested in your *Sud Ouest* connection. Don't you have things to show me?"

Martine, in a checked black-and-white wool suit, reached into her matching soft leather briefcase. She set two folders of printouts next to the ashtray and flicked ash from her cigarette. "Makes for interesting reading. I culled the highlights. My contact ran a search up to the present. Thin, but all they had."

She pointed to the other file with her red-lacquered nail. "Euskadi Action. Not a group a mother wants her daughter involved with, according to my source. A radical offshoot faction of ETA. But I didn't have time to read it."

Aimée picked the cigarette from Martine's fingers, took a deep drag. The nicotine jolt went right to her head.

Martine took back her cigarette. "You quit."

"I'm always quitting." Aimée tapped her heeled boots.

Martine exhaled a stream of blue smoke. "Prada boots. Nice."

"Borrowed them from you, remember?"

"No wonder." Martine leaned back, cocked her head. "Who is he?"

Aimée sighed. She could never keep anything from Martine. "That obvious?"

"You're glowing." Martine grinned. "For once, you're following my advice. In a way. Knowing you, *une aventure*, the one-night kind?"

"The *flic*."

"Lean over: time for a spanking," Martine said, crushing out her cigarette. "Never learn, do you?" But Aimée saw the wheels spinning in Martine's head; a job, possible advancement. "So he was good, eh, like last time?"

A pang went through her. Too good. "I don't trust him."

"He's married?"

"In divorce proceedings, custody issues." She took a cigarette from Martine's pack of Murattis. "But that's not why."

Martine lit her cigarette. "I'm listening."

So she told her. Everything. Like she had since they were sixteen.

"Sounds like Melac's watching his back, wants to keep his job, make alimony payments." Martine shrugged. "So either keep it physical or ignore his calls."

"Morbier said trust no one."

"He's right," Martine said. "In his situation, I'd say the same."

Once a leak sprang, it watered everything. But she had an idea. "How's your sister's husband's cousin?"

Martine glanced at her watch, set some francs on the counter. "The half-deaf one with the hots for you? Florent?"

"That's him. I forgot his name."

"Still half-deaf, still has the hots for you," she said. "As usual, he asked after you last Sunday at dinner. Promoted, I think."

Even better. Florent worked in an administrative branch of the RG. She couldn't remember which one. "Then I should take him out to lunch."

"Don't play with him, Aimée. He's naïve."

"And he's forty-five years old, a grown man still living with his mother."

"I know what you're thinking." Martine's eyes narrowed. "You'd use him to find what the RG has on this woman's involvement with ETA?"

"Put that way, no. I couldn't." She averted her eyes. "But the woman Morbier loved was murdered and he's the suspect; who knows what they've done to him. He's protecting his informer, something to do with his case in Lyon, so he's got no alibi. I need to find her murderer."

"Makes a kind of logic," Martine said. "But the ETA connection's a stretch. A twenty-year stretch."

"Somewhere to start, Martine."

"Somewhere to dead-end, quick." Martine picked up her bag. "See for yourself tonight. Join me. As I said, I'm covering the Basque minister's announcement of the agreement. You'd get to see a princess and find out how defused ETA's become. ETA's bombings alienated their old power base; people want no more violence. Meet the man, listen; he'll tell you."

Out on the windswept street, the drizzle had stopped. The

Métro thundered by overhead. Martine checked her much-used Vuitton agenda. "Time for my news feature. All seven minutes of it."

Martine gestured to the distant sphere-like aluminum-coated Radio France building, referred to by all as the Camembert. "Awful, *non?* Five kilometers of snaking corridors and half the time I'm lost. See you tonight, Musée Marmottan, six-thirty."

Now she could check out Euskadi Action's demonstration at the same time.

Martine hurried over the cobbles and turned the corner. The wind picked up, scattering shriveled leaves from the gutter. The roar of the Métro receded as it crossed the Seine.

A few low dark clouds threatened rain. Aimée left her scooter protected under the arched metal Métro supports and climbed the steep, narrow Passage des Eaux, pinched in a deep groove between tall limestone buildings. Wide enough for two-legged creatures. Just. A lone glass lantern on a curled metal rod hung like a stubborn raindrop determined not to fall. She looked beyond the deep butterscotch walls in the crackling, hard autumn light paling on the roof tiles.

Stupid to sleep with Melac. And to like it. She wanted to kick herself. Panting, she reached the last step and stood atop Passy. Beyond the passage summit loomed the Trocadéro hill on the right. Below lay two-story buildings and flashes of green: back courtyards and streets threading the old village, widening in places and reverting to the original horse-cart dimensions. No hint of the stone vaulted cellars and passages underneath, honeycombing ancient quarry tunnels. Hidden, covered, like everything else so far.

The sky opened and she ran for shelter.

\* \* \*

IN THE ROOM the Balzac museum pamphlet described as his "study," Aimée paused at Balzac's simple wood writing desk. At least the place was dry, the heater worked, and quiet reigned until the next tour of this labyrinthine series of small rooms—a strange place where one entered on the third floor, then descended a corkscrew staircase to the first. Like entering the neck of wine bottle.

But a place in which to think. Figure out Melac's angle. At *La Crim*, she'd seen his empty desk. The receptionist confirmed he'd taken leave. But a leave of two days, as he'd said? Or two weeks? She couldn't be sure. There was no guarantee in the sweet talk of this man who'd put her under investigation last month.

Morbier's cryptic comment about the leaking robinet in the jail's visiting room made sense now. A leak. A leak in the force.

Knowing Morbier, he was keeping something close to his chest. He could have been putting on a show for watching eyes in the visiting room. Just like him.

Her mind went to the secrets he was keeping from her, hinted at by a gesture, a word when he was unaware. This gray past buried deep. As if she didn't know. Didn't suspect what had really happened to her father. Or her mother. Every time she'd asked, his answer had been to tell her to leave the past alone.

She paused by the window overlooking the narrow, walled back lane. The heater hissed, emitting puffs of warmth. In the terra-cotta vase, an arrangement of burnt orange-red maple leaves glowed in the light. But the maple leaves provided no answers.

Nor did the bust of Balzac with his opaque marble stare. A debt-ridden Balzac had rented rooms here in Passy, then a village outside Paris. Hounded by creditors, he'd often had to escape out the back door and down the lane. In spite of this, he'd written much of his early nineteenth-century saga, the many-volumed *Comédie Humaine*, and drunk fifty cups of coffee a day at this gouged wooden desk. She could relate to that.

She chewed her lip, trying to face the fear that was making her insides shiver. She kept reliving Melac's appearance in the hallway, his nuzzled kisses along her neck, his insistence on knowing her feelings, his curiosity about the phone call. The probing of his gray eyes.

She didn't do *flics*. Simple. She'd ignore the way he'd made her feel, his warm legs entwined with hers under the sheets, this talk of a "relationship."

No mistaking the veiled panic in Morbier's voice. He needed her help. The little he'd given her—a leak, an informer he couldn't name—didn't point her to Xavierre's murderer. Unless a bent *flic* had murdered her to put blame on Morbier and derail his investigation. She doubted that. But this Lyon case, this leak? She put that aside for now.

She had to concentrate on the info Martine had given her on Xavierre's background. Find a link, figure out if it led anywhere. Her father had always said think like the perp; if you don't know the perp, go to the suspect; no suspect, back to basics—the victim.

In the Balzac museum's narrow reading room, she opened Xavierre's file. Reading from the faxed newspaper articles dating from 1974, a whole other aspect of Xavierre Contrexo emerged. Student ETA activist and supporter, implicated in a bombing in Navarre that claimed a policeman's life. Along with two other students: Timo Baptista, and a man simply referred to in the newspaper as Agustino.

The painter. No wonder he regretted the past and devoted himself to painting and making peace his life's work now.

She sat back, wondering if this Timo Baptista had taken the oath, too, and served time in prison. Morbier's words rang in her head. The trio from Bayonne. Had he known of Xavierre's ETA past?

According to the next article, also dated 1974, Xavierre's lawyer, d'Eslay, bright and from a wealthy family, had found mitigating circumstances, and there was a retrial. Xavierre had served seven months in total. A later article mentioned they had married and had one daughter. Then the only mentions were of the Basque cultural and art society fund-raisers and society events over the years, of Bayonne and Paris charity functions. A divorce. His last year's obituary in *Sud Ouest*.

A wild youth, then a 180-degree turnaround to patroness of the arts, of Basque culture. From all appearances, Xavierre had changed and led a different life.

Not much progress or an arrow pointing to a tie-in with ETA today. Yet Agustino, Xavierre's old compadre, hadn't told her the whole story. Why not?

Right away, she'd sensed he was hiding something. His reluctance, admitted "cowardice," causing him to avoid facing Irati, stuck in the back of her mind.

She'd question Agustino again. Still, no tie-in to Xavierre's murder.

Next she phoned Florent at the RG. After two calls, she reached his office. "Monsieur Florent's attending the Strasbourg conference, Mademoiselle," the saccharine-voiced secretary told her.

"Until when?"

"Monsieur Florent's on holiday after that. Returns middle of the month, Mademoiselle. A cruise."

With his mother, no doubt.

She left her number just in case he returned.

Her arrows hit no targets, no return calls with respect to the Mercedes or Irati's triangulated cell phone line. She sat back in the chair, shoulders slumped, rubbing her neck.

So far she'd left messages and learned Xavierre had been involved with ETA years ago and had an RG file. And she'd slept with Melac, whom she didn't trust. His citrus scent was still in her hair. Thank god Balzac's bust was the only witness.

The second file on Euskadi Action contained stapled articles and clippings. One printout dated two months ago from the Basque Watch security newsletter got her attention.

Bylined in the article was ETA's motto *Bietan jarrai*, "Keep up on both," illustrated by ETA's trademark symbol of a snake—representing politics—wrapped around an ax—representing armed fight. A little shudder ran through her. Headlined FRENCH BASQUE *ETTARAS* AFFILIATED WITH ETA, the article pointed to a logistical network of *ettara* in France using a pool of mostly youths scattered across the Pays Basque who were willing to engage in missions under ETA's political guise.

> French and Spanish police seek to reduce ETA's capability by banning the political wing of the movement, which seeks an independent, autonomous Basque state. The logic to banning the political wing, which has operated for the last decade under different names—Euskadi Action the most recent—is that both wings are inextricably linked.
>
> Banning the political branch, authorities hope, would reduce the flow of funds and support to the militant units or *ettaras* of Euskadi Action. Yet other authorities disagree, arguing a ban would stimulate

robberies used to fund ETA operations along with "revolutionary taxes" exacted on local businesses under the guise of protection.

No one knows just how far the covert organization extends. Authorities estimate the *ettara* active in France using false passports and identities—members who are trained to kill and who work in cells of four people—could number a hundred youths.

Not a comforting thought. Her mind went to the *Imprimerie Nationale* heist, figuring it was connected. After all, to travel, to operate, one needed ID. Hard to find hundreds of clean passports for an activist group any other way. And profit by selling the surplus to fund operations.

She scanned the next article, from January 1992, focused on GAL, the dirty war. The article gave background on France's vaunted tradition of a haven, an asylum for political dissidents, citing Lenin, Trotsky, and the Ayatollah Khomeini. Notably, since the Spanish Civil War in the thirties, it had been a sanctuary for refugees from Franco's dictatorship, and the tradition continued into the eighties of providing political-refugee status for ETA militants, even refusing Spanish extradition demands.

But things changed, she noted, with the "dirty war."

From 1983 through 1987 forty attacks on French soil by GAL, Grupos Antiterroristas de Liberación, mercenaries hired by high Spanish officials, shot, kidnapped and blew up ETA members and innocent French bystanders. Responsibility extended to the highest offices in Madrid's ministry. GAL mercenaries crossed the French border to wage war on refugee ETA members, and on French civilians thought to collude.

More than ten years later, with new disclosures and impending GAL trials of high military officials, ETA violence renewed with *ettaras* enlisted from disaffected youths. Known activities include sabotaging rail lines for a new high speed train from France to Spain. The planned route, a Y shape with 80% of the rail lines underground, runs aboveground the rest of the way through the Basque countryside. Authorities dismiss the sabotage as tactics by local business, under the cloak of ETA, to reroute commerce to their area.

The next article, dated the previous week, a stilted translation, led further:

This year in continuing reverberations from the revelations of high-placed security officials on trial suspected of organized vigilantism under the auspices of GAL, the dirty war, ETA's attacks have escalated.

The airing of the state-sponsored GAL, "dirty war," scheme in the early 1990s led to a political scandal in Spain.

Reactions to those attacks have caused an ideological split within ETA between those who refuse to condone violence and those who support armed struggle. The shift from general support for ETA showed during the election of former ETA sympathizing with Goikoetxea, a French Basque assemblyman from Navarre, who engineered the referendum recently passed by a narrow margin.

So Goikoetxea's formal announcement tonight of the referendum agreement had faced dissent in broken ranks. Serious enough to spur the *ettaras*?

If Martine had had the time to read this, her tune would have changed.

Still, what did that have to do with Xavierre's murder? Why now, on the eve of her daughter's wedding?

But Irati's connection, slim if anything, existed. Covert operations required money. A network needed funds to operate safe houses, to purchase arms. Irati, with the town house in the 16th and her inheritance from a successful, rich father, represented a small fortune.

Could Irati have sympathized with Euskadi Action, attended meetings, even donated, been put on the mailing list? An unwitting accomplice? Forced by . . . by what?

"In the next room, we see Balzac's genealogical chart of *La Comédie Humaine*," said a guide leading a group of middle-aged couples, educated retirees by the look of their culture-vulture guidebooks and high-end anoraks. Part of a culture tour, so popular with active retirees who boned up on history for educational dinners with their grandchildren or to impress their belote playing partners.

"On this chart, illustrated by Balzac himself, he outlines the saga's chronology, with an amazing and detailed fictional character family tree. The interrelatedness by marriage, dalliances, friendships, village and clan ties, love triangles, tied by oaths, connecting . . ." the guide droned on.

Aimée looked up. Tied by oath. Agustino's words.

Her cell vibrated in her pocket. "*Allô?*"

"Irati's on the phone," Léo said. "She's on the move, too."

At last. Aimée scooped up the printouts and slipped them in her bag.

"No cell phones allowed, *shhh.*" Poking her head around the corner, the guide, a white-haired, pert-nosed woman with frameless designer glasses, frowned. She pointed to the sign. "You're disturbing our tour."

Aimée nodded, rushing to the stairs. "Can I listen, Léo?"

"My equipment's not hooked up for second-party relay," Léo said. "But I'd say she's in a car."

"What's she saying, Léo?"

"Too much interference, fading in and out of dead zones. Doesn't sound French."

Aimée stiffened. "Basque?"

"Sounds Greek to me. But I can give you her geographic coordinates."

High-pitched bleeping noises punctuated by intermittent blips sounded in the background.

"Hold on, Léo."

With the phone to her ear, she took the narrow stairs two at time, crossed the tree-lined courtyard, and went up more stairs to rue Raynouard. Not two blocks from Xavierre's, yet still several blocks from her parked scooter.

"Her tracking signal's emitting on rue de Passy."

"Cross street?"

"Looks like Boulainvilliers Métro."

*Merde!* Blocks away.

"Keep talking, Léo." A biting wind hit her cheekbones. She wrapped her scarf tighter around her neck, plugged in her earbuds, stuck the phone in her pocket, and ran.

By the time she reached her scooter, she was out of breath. She pulled the scooter off its kickstand and keyed the ignition.

"I'm at Passy Métro. Which way?"

"Go north to Trocadéro."

She gunned the scooter, the wheels bumping over the cobbled street.

After climbing the Trocadéro hill, she saw the bland white wall of the Passy cemetery. "I'm at Trocadéro . . . the Passy cemetery?"

"The signal's moving down rue de la Pompe."

Aimée turned left, shifted into second gear. She wove among the buses, faster now, flying over the zebra-striped crosswalks.

"She's passing Lycée Janson de Sailly."

The elite Catholic high school was several blocks ahead. Aimée swerved to avoid a sweeping street cleaner. Aimée tried to think where she was headed: Shop? A market? "What's nearby, Léo?" A gust of leaves swirled by her feet from the gutter. Horns blared.

"On the map, Marché Saint-Didier," Léo said.

"Can't you pinpoint her caller's location, the number?" Aimée asked, breathless.

"If she stays on long enough," Léo said. "All my other scanners are monitoring work-related contracts right now."

In other words, the military. And Léo needed another scanner to pinpoint Irati's caller's number and location.

Irati would be driving a Mercedes, the other dark-colored one from the driveway. But that described every other car in this neighborhood. Straining now, her breath vaporous in the chill mid-morning air, she veered right onto rue Saint-Didier.

A block down, she saw the rose-brick–covered Marché Saint-Didier. Locals with string bags clogged the pavement. A Mercedes was backing up into a crosswalk. Aimée braked, hopped off, and pulled her scooter near the lamp post.

A gray Renault came to an abrupt stop on her left. Two men jumped out. From the look of their short hair, nondescript dark blue windbreakers, and thick-soled black shoes, undercover *flics*. Or a special forces terrorist branch.

Aimée didn't have time to figure this out, much less to speculate about how they'd known and gotten here so fast. She had to warn Irati, use this chance to get information from her.

Irati, wearing a long dark chocolate wool coat and boots, carrying a full Printemps shopping bag, hurried across the narrow street and into the crowd. Morning shoppers thronged the entrance.

Aimée followed her; she had to reach Irati before these men got to her. The playing field had shifted, but she didn't know how.

"No signal, Aimée."

"Got her, Léo. *Merci.*"

Aimée lowered her head and followed. The two men split up, and Aimée reached for the phone in her pocket.

She hit Irati's number.

"Two men followed you, Irati," Aimée said. "They're entering the market."

"You again? Leave me alone." Pause. "You're lying."

"Turn around. See the one in the blue windbreaker?"

A gasp of air. She'd seen him. "You had me followed . . . why?"

"No, not me," she said. "You're being watched."

"But who are they?" Irati's voice quavered.

"*Flics*, special forces, who knows? But before you find out," she said, "tell me where you're meeting the Basques."

"But you. . . ." Irati stumbled. "How in the world . . . ?" she caught herself.

But not in time. She hadn't denied she was meeting the Basques.

"Trust me, Irati," she said. "I'm trying to help you, to find out who murdered your mother. What do they want?"

The line buzzed. Irati had hung up.

Aimée ran past counters of hanging red string sausages, life-less beady-eyed rabbits suspended upside down, and displays of winter melons. Milling shoppers lined the aisles in the cavern-ous iron-strutted market hall. Shouts of "fresh Bresse chicken" came from a butcher in a bloodstained apron, along with scents of rosemary and fennel from the herb counter.

No Irati.

Think. Given the phone call, a "meet" set up in a crowded market, Irati's options narrowed. Damned if she didn't meet their demands, damned if she led the *flics* to them. In Irati's posi-tion, she'd get the hell out.

One of the blue windbreakers stood by the cheese counter, the other near the sample segments of glistening orange clemen-tines behind an iron column. They were ignoring the first rule of shadowing, the rules her father had taught her: never attempt to hide. No doubt they'd break the others too: keep behind the suspect, act naturally no matter what, and never meet the sus-pect's eye. But she wasn't going to wait to find out.

Aimée walked backward in the crowd, mingling in the stream to avoid attention. At the entrance, she turned and hurried like everyone else. A rear side entrance exited on rue Mesnil. In the distance she saw the back of Irati's coat, already three quarters of the way to Place Victor Hugo. Almost a block ahead.

Aimée took off, her boot heels echoing off the tall limestone buildings lining the street. The sharp wind made tears form in her eyes. And then Irati had turned the corner.

Aimée pumped her legs. Ran as fast as she could. A minute later, she rounded the corner. Place Victor Hugo shone in the weak sunlight, a roundabout with ten streets radiating from it like the spokes of bicycle wheels. And no Irati.

*Wednesday Midday*

IN THE HUMID vaulted visiting room, Morbier wiped his neck with a stained handkerchief.

"Life's a tightwire, high above the circus crowd: any moment, you risk falling," said Lucard, the *juge d'instruction*. "But I don't need to tell you that, Morbier."

Lucard tented his slim fingers, trained his beady black eyes on the ceiling, and emitted a sigh.

Lucard had always reminded Morbier of a crow, scanning for shiny bright things in the gutter. After all, that was his job, so why shouldn't he resemble a scavenger?

"The IGS insists on extending your time in the *garde à vue*. They asked for my opinion," Lucard said. "A formality, of course."

Another twenty-four hours in this hellhole. No chance of reaching Laguardiere, or finding Xavierre's killer. A shame, too, since he'd worked with Lucard, a tough, thorough examining magistrate despite his youth, stylishly tousled hair, and Grandes Écoles bearing. He'd turned out to be just another lackey, a pin-stripe suit in the system.

"Think I'm a flight risk, Lucard?"

"Liken it to the balancing act between the past and present," said Lucard. "Keeping to the tightrope analogy, you reach the wire by

"Our branch would appreciate your cooperation."

Meaning they were as desperate and clueless as she was?

"My father never mentioned you," she said, stalling, thinking of the implications. Morbier's words played in her head: "Trust no one." Had they screwed her father? And were about to do the same to Morbier?

"Think about it, Mademoiselle Leduc," he said. "I'll be in touch. Don't worry, I can always find you."

She tried to control her shaking hands as she passed back the phone. The man's bland expression didn't change.

The men piled into the car. She watched until the brake lights turned the corner.

"Whatever you said . . ." Martine swallowed. ". . . worked."

"The EPIGN wants to recruit me."

Martine blinked.

"He asked me to think about it," she said.

An hour, a day? she wondered.

"Rumor goes they make it impossible for you to refuse."

Like her father? "Not my thing, Martine."

"Think of it this way, Aimée," Martine said. "The EPIGN's active in Basque territory. Even have a HALO detachment specializing in VIP protection." Martine shot her a look. "But it was sloppy work allowing the kidnapping. Matter of fact, they blew it. Figures. All that training on emergency response goes to their head. Now they need you."

"But I screwed up, Martine," she said. "I didn't protect Xavierre. Her murder's connected. She's the link. Now the princess."

"Put it in perspective," Martine said. "ETA needs to prove the princess is alive. That's the first step in any negotiation. This could take days, make for a nice long feature."

Aimée didn't return Martine's grin.

"It's your *derrière* you need to watch." Martine handed Aimée a tissue. "Clean up your mascara: you've got raccoon eyes."

Aimée wet the tissue with her tongue and dabbed under her eyes. And the wheels clicked. The museum surveillance cameras. She scanned the museum's entrance, but the cameras were obscured by hanging branches. Another look revealed that the town house cameras opposite were trained in other directions.

"But the cameras would have caught the kidnapping."

Martine shrugged. "The princess was a no-show. Nothing on tape."

*Merde.* She'd wasted time already, and she needed backup. She pulled out her phone and spoke to her cousin Sebastian, arranging to meet in twenty minutes.

She keyed her scooter's ignition.

"The ambassador agreed to sign a vaguely worded promise," Martine said. "But no way can he or the girl's father authorize a prison release just like that. Or snap their fingers and hold a new election."

Martine lit a cigarette. Smoke hovered, dissipating under the bare branches like mist. "Aimée, find me another angle to this kidnapping."

"Doesn't sit right, does it?" Aimée pulled on her Blue Fever helmet. Oil-slicked rainbow puddles bled into the cracks between the uneven cobbles.

Martine nodded. "If this Basque agreement ties somehow to Xavierre's murder, and Agustino knew . . . ?"

"Martine, he knows something, but—"

"He's a small fish," Martine interrupted. "I want the big fish. Trust me," she said. "That *mec*, by the way, the charmer without expression?"

Aimée nodded. Monsieur Blandface.

"Warned me off the story." Martine ground the cigarette out with her toe. "Thinks he can muzzle the press? Not me. But you're on to something: there's more to this. The way I write this up . . . well, if you find me ammunition, I'll load it Morbier's way. But I need proof, *compris?* Why should those boys have their sick fun?"

Aimée wished that made her feel better. She revved the engine, popped into first, and took off into the night.

*Wednesday Evening*

MARIA STRUGGLED, TRYING to see through the grainy darkness of the burlap bag over her head. Cold dampness sent shivers up her arms, bare but for her spaghetti-strap silk mini. She strained to hear, listening for traffic or voices, but heard only the echoing of footsteps. Hers and another.

Then a low, short toot. The recognizable whistle of a barge. The smell of algae. They were by the Seine.

She tripped on metal pipes, losing her balance and sending them clanging and rolling. Hands jerked her bound wrists behind her.

"Get up!"

Trussed and bound like a pig, she couldn't move sideways. Or yell with her mouth duct-taped shut. She kicked out her foot and hit a pipe.

Sharp pain shot up her leg. And the terror she'd tried to fight took over. Hot, panicked breaths from her nose filled the bag with warm suffocating air. She couldn't breathe. Couldn't open her mouth.

She felt herself rolled over, pulled upright, leaned against wet freezing metal. The bag was pulled off her head.

Water dripped from a broken pipe, and puddles reflected the

sputtering glow of a kerosene lamp. The reek of kerosene and mildew was everywhere. A man leaned over the lamp, adjusted the flame brighter. She gasped at his face. Silhouetted against the darkness, a blood-soaked bandage covered his eye.

She felt a searing stinging as he ripped the duct tape from her mouth. Her lips were raw, and chunks of her black hair had been pulled out. Her eyes teared and her body shook with cold.

"Where's Lucas . . . where am I?"

No answer.

"Let's pretend this didn't happen. Take my bag." She turned her face away. "I didn't see you. I don't know you."

"But you already have." She heard the accent, the Basque way of saying *b* for a *t*, the *r* turning into *err*. He squatted next to her on the flaking rusted pipes. "Be a good girl. Do what I say."

"You've got to let me go." Her voice rose. This wasn't happening. Couldn't happen. "The ambassador will raise hell if I'm not back. I won't say anything."

He took a pistol from his brown leather jacket pocket. "Do I have to use this?"

She gulped. Shaking, she couldn't stop shaking, or her teeth from chattering. She'd lost her shoes, her stockings were ripped, and her bare feet were going numb from the cold.

"What do you want?"

He turned away.

"Don't you understand they're expecting me? I'll get in trouble."

Like the last time.

He gave a small smile. "You don't call this trouble?"

She let out a scream. Screamed again and again. Only the piercing echoes from the steel rafters responded.

"No one can hear you," he said. "Quit moving."

"I c-c-can't, too cold."

"Call this cold?" He snorted. "Try living a winter in the mountains. Wind like ice cutting over the Pyrénées, through the valley, and only boiled snow to drink."

A Basque. That didn't stop her shaking. Her memories of the Basque country came from summers in her friend's mother's village. Pine branches heavy with rain, their crisp scent wafting over the whitewashed farmhouses and red-tiled roofs bordering the green sheep meadows. Not this bone-chilling, damp-permeated, rusting warehouse.

He was a fine one to talk. He wore a jacket, boots, and wool scarf. Her dress was soaked, a copper-tinged reeking mess. What did he expect? She was without a coat.

"B-b-but you've got warm clothes."

"Complaining?"

At the look on his face, she tried to make herself small. Fear coursed through her veins. "*Non.*"

"Prove it. Can you?"

She nodded.

He unzipped his jacket, threw it on her shaking bare legs. "You sew?"

Nonplussed, she stared, shivering.

He unwound the blood-soaked bandage covering his eye. Pulled the kerosene lantern closer. She gasped. Clotted blood surrounded his bruised left eye, which was swollen shut. His shirt collar was stained dark with blood.

He reached over and untied her hands. She inhaled a metallic whiff of blood, his perspiration.

"Use this." He handed her a travel-sized sewing kit. A small bottle of liqueur, airplane-sized, and a white embroidered towel. "Clean it right."

She didn't want to touch him.

"Or I use this."

One hand held the gun; the other pulled back the matted black hair from his temple.

She winced. "Bring the light closer so I can see."

The kerosene lantern scraped over the stained concrete floor.

Black slivers studded his eyelid; deep red cuts scored the edge of his eye. She sucked in air. "I need tweezers."

"Eh? Just clean and sew it up."

"But there are pieces of something in there. If you don't take them out, you'll get an infection. Now if I had my bag with twee . . . zers. . . ." Her teeth chattered again.

He reached over, took her vanilla leather Birkin bag, and dumped out the contents: her new Vuitton wallet, agenda, checkbook, receipts, key ring, and cell phone tumbled on the rust flakes.

Her cell phone.

Her hopes lifted. A chance now. She'd help him, gain his confidence, and call for help.

"Check the side pocket for the tweezers," she said. "Beside my lipstick."

She pulled his jacket around her legs, glanced up. Giant tarnished metal cranes loomed over them, suspended in the air, like giraffes caught in flight. A slanted industrial glass roof above what looked like an assembly line. Wheels and rubber conveyor belts strewn on the floor. A familiar insignia with an R molded into one of the iron pillars.

R for Renault. She realized they were in the derelict Renault auto works on Île Seguin. The old production plant on the outskirts covered the island in the Seine. It had been abandoned for years. She'd gone by the plant countless times on the way to school when her father was posted to the Paris embassy. As a little girl she'd watched the finished cars loaded onto barges, fascinated.

She had to get her phone. Give the location. Grab a taxi and slip in the embassy back door, no one the wiser.

She poured the liqueur on the tweezers and over his cheek-bone. He made a light intake of breath. Considering the blood he'd lost, he should be ready to pass out.

He grabbed the bottle, took a long drink. Then another.

If he passed out drunk, even better.

"Hurry up."

She got to work. Instead of clubbing, she found herself in a freezing abandoned auto works swabbing a terrorist's wound. But she had a plan.

"My friend's mother's people come from Basse Navarre," she said, chewing the thread off with her teeth, determined to make conversation, relax him and lull him to carelessness. "Know it?"

"Why?" His chest muscles flexed. Hard. He grabbed her hair.

"Oww . . . your accent's like her uncle's. That's all."

"Rich brat, what do you know?" He relaxed the grip on her hair. "What's this?" He picked up papers from her bag, her student card mired in the puddle. He stared at it. "You study?"

"No, I'm just a spoiled brat shopping and lunching with my girlfriends." Anger flushed her cheeks. "I take design courses. Function in architecture. Model a bit on the side. Not. . . ." She stopped before she said "a kidnapper like you."

"Impressive. Maybe you'll give me design tips."

He nudged her with the gun.

Feeling more confident now, she tried to keep the conversation going. "I'm moving in with my boyfriend next year."

"Does your father know?"

"My boyfriend's a photographer," she said. "An artist."

"Art's political."

What did that mean? Art went on the wall. "Ready?" She probed deep with the tweezers.

He squinted, closing his eyes, his teeth grinding.

Her pink phone gleamed in the beams of kerosene light just a reach away. She edged toward it.

His left hand grabbed hers in a grip like steel.

"What's this?" Her tweezers held a blackened sliver of sharp metal.

"Shrapnel." The lines in his brow relaxed. "Take it all out." He drank more.

"Shrapnel . . . you mean from a bullet?"

Horrified, she dropped the tweezers, which clattered on the wet cement.

"Did you kill someone?"

He leaned back, still pointing the gun at her. "Struggle has to be seen within the political context," he said. "There are people who choose nonviolent struggle; and then us, who have another vision and use other tactics."

He'd never before said so many words in a sentence. He reminded her of her friend's uncle, a stocky farmer with long ears who was short on conversation.

"The government outlaws the Basques' right to decide our future," he said. "No one wants violence. But struggle demands sacrifice."

She'd seen the bombings on the *télé*. The rehearsed speeches and demands by men in ski masks with guns. Like him.

"But deep down, you can't mean you'd shoot—"

"Ask the seven hundred prisoners held in Spanish jails, the corrupt French *flics* who rule Basse Navarre," he interrupted, letting out a deep breath. "Or ask my brother. Tortured. My father. A cripple for life."

She didn't know what to say.

"But the law . . . ?"

"Welcome to the real world," he said sarcastically. "It gets down and dirty outside the palace."

"What palace? My father works. So does my mother."

An awful fear filled her. What if Lucas and these terrorists meant to hold her for ransom?

"Take the pieces of shrapnel out. Now." He held the gun, his fingers looser. His Adam's apple bobbed. She rubbed her hands in the cold. Trying not to look at her phone. So close. How with one little reach . . . maybe with her toe. . . .

He growled. "What are you waiting for?"

She hid her disgust. Coating crime with politics got no sympathy from her. Just a renegade, like all the bandits, those smugglers high in the Basse Navarre. A Basque stronghold. Since time immemorial, holing up in remote villages, banding together, spitting in the eye of authority and the government. Robbing pilgrims, the innocent, the desperate, whether they were fleeing from the Inquisition, the Bourbons, or the Nazis along the ancient paths and escape routes through the Pyrénées.

"Pull more splinters out, understand?" he said, gasping in pain.

Her breaths frosted in the air. She edged her numb foot forward. Further. Her big toe touched the pink casing.

Loud crashing noises. Then the tramp of boots.

"Why the hell didn't you answer?" asked a gravel-voiced man in a black ski mask.

Terror gripped her. Another man leaned down, riffling

through the strewn contents of her bag. Grabbed her cell phone. "Pink?"

Mud rimmed his boots. The mixed smell of earth and algae as he kicked the bloody bandages. "Letting her play doctor, Joxi?" he said. "And messy. I don't like messy."

The gravel-voiced one gestured to the *mec*. "Pick this up. All of it."

Panic sliced across her like a blade.

Joxi groaned and fell back.

"Time for a real doctor." His black eyes glittered behind the eyeholes in the mask. "Tape her back up. Put her in the van."

"W-wh-where?" Her voice chattered with cold.

He looked at her, back at the other *mec*, and just laughed.

*Wednesday Evening*

MIST HOVERED LOW over the hedgerows, silent and damp. A gust of wind stirred the dead leaves. Not even a twitter came from the bushes. A wave of relief passed over her as she saw Sebastian's secondhand van, a Berlingo, at the curb.

She switched off the scooter's ignition, pulled off her helmet, and noticed a run in her black stockings. A new pair, too.

"Tool set, like you ordered, all loaded in back," Sebastian said.

Sebastian, her younger cousin, stood a head taller than Aimée. He sported a wool cap over his dark blond hair, jeans and a hand-knit fisherman's sweater accentuating his lean frame. A former junkie, he'd been clean for several years.

"You've put on weight, Sebastian," she said.

A good sign.

"Blame it on Regula's fondue, and the raclette."

His new girlfriend Regula, Swiss and steady, cooked with the *chefs collectifs,* which put on roving underground gourmet events. Exclusive and only by word of mouth.

"The framing shop business good?"

Sebastian had expanded his framing business to a third shop. She'd cosigned the loan. He owed her.

"Orders and more orders." He grinned. "I've only got an hour."

"No problem." She squeezed his arm. "I'm happy for you."

She helped him load her scooter into the back of his van. "Ready. You remember how to dust for prints?"

"There's a Web site, Aimée."

Like for everything now.

At Agustino's she didn't know what they'd find. But they'd find something.

He gunned his van down Avenue Mozart. Skeleton-branched chestnut trees shuddered in the wind.

"All over this *quartier* you see neo-Cubist architecture fighting the flourishes of Art Nouveau," Sebastian said. "Neo-Cubism speaks to the Bauhaus and Gropius influence." He pointed out his open window, respect in his voice. "Between the wars, 'the style international' was the hit at the Decorative Arts Exposition in 1925."

She stared at Sebastian. "My little cousin knows Bauhaus from a *boudin* sausage?"

"Courtesy of my client on neighboring rue de l'Assomption," Sebastian replied. "When I called Bauhaus a *très* cool DJ, he set me straight. He's a real Mallet-Stevens buff."

Aimée pointed to a spot in the lane. "Park it here."

She grabbed two flashlights and handed him one. "Let's go."

She retraced her steps from yesterday past the almost-hidden Fondation Le Corbusier annex sign.

Sebastian's work boots crunched on the gravel and packed dirt. Secluded darkness, a perfect place to hide. She shivered.

The damp bushes trembled in the gentle wind. A quiet breeze rippled the sparse carpet of brown leaves. The derelict *hôtel particulier* was a dark shadow in the background. Ahead, Agustino's lit atelier was like a beacon.

She wished she'd worn wool socks and Doc Martens like Sebastian, instead of high-heeled Prada boots. Skittering noises and thumping came from the tree branches overhead.

Sebastian hissed. "Over there."

Something darted in the glistening wet hedgerow. A shadow moved on the white stone wall separating the atelier from the garden. Startled, she felt Sebastian grab her arm, shove her down in the wet grass.

*Wednesday Night*

MARIA SHIVERED IN the bone-chilling cold. The jacket over her torn silk chemise offered little protection from the dampness. She couldn't distinguish night or day in the stone-vaulted cavern. She knew she was underground somewhere, her purse and phone gone. Periodic pumping sounds came from above, punctuated by the whine of a bell. Hours ago she'd heard ducks quacking, caught the odor of water, before the men herded her, with the bag over her head, down a sloping ramp.

Now she saw a line of electric lights receding down the long tunnel, shadows in cell-like caverns like the one she huddled in now, chained to the metal pipe.

Voices murmured in a mixture of Basque and French. She could pick out words, part of a phrase, but they were speaking a rural dialect.

"You worry too much" came from one with a gravelly, grating voice. "The Gestapistes used it. No one heard the screams down here."

Her heart thumped, looking around at the blackened stone. A Gestapo torture chamber? She didn't doubt it.

Her bare feet skittered on the loose pebbles and crumbling

plaster. How could she escape? What had happened to the wounded one they called Joxi?

"Fascinating, eh, the underground." The *mec* wearing blue trousers and work jacket stood still in his ski mask. "Historic. Like the caves in my valley." He handed her a rag, acting solicitous. "Wipe those eyes, eh. Cooperate and you go home."

Her chained hands reached for the rag.

He tore the duct tape off her mouth with a loud rip. Her eyes blinked, tearing with pain from her raw skin.

"You'll let me go?"

"Behave, or it goes back on."

It would anyway. But they needed her alive.

"What . . . what do you want?"

"Read this. Word for word." He thrust the card at her.

She shivered. "Did anyone . . . get killed?"

"Not yet."

Liar.

He checked the time. Pulled out a small tape recorder.

"Read just what it says."

Garbage. Lies. She spit and it landed on his sleeve.

"Full of spirit, eh? Better speak better than you aim."

He wiped his arm. Reached for a hunting knife with a bone handle and ran the tip along her chin. "That's if you want to live."

She struggled to kick her feet, but her ankles were taped.

"Read it, Princess, a simple thing. Then you're free, back home like you never left."

"Bombing buildings, shootings . . . all that violence goes nowhere," she said, gasping for breath. "Didn't you learn that in the eighties? That's *passé* . . . the Basques I know want peace—"

"*Et alors*, you're a patriot," he interrupted. "Like us." Only his dark eyes were visible behind the ski mask. "But if you don't read, you die, others die. What will that prove?"

Her shoulders shook. Fear rippled her insides.

"So, Princess?" The cold knife tip touched her chin bone.

A steady drip, drip, drip came from the corner. She took a breath and read: "I support and advocate the autonomy of the Basque region. And ask my father to do the same." Her throat caught. He pressed the knife tip harder against her chin. Somehow she made herself keep reading. "Not only should there be cultural centers teaching Basque history and language, but there must be the release of all Basque prisoners, and a new referendum."

She stifled a sob.

He hit STOP, rubbed his neck, impatient now. "Keep reading. Convince your father." He moved the knife blade to the jugular vein in her bare white throat. "Talk."

He hit RECORD.

She stumbled a few times but continued to the end.

"You think I'm a bargaining chip, a means to some end?" Her lip trembled. "Kidnapping me won't give Basques autonomy. Don't you understand?"

He stuck the duct tape back on her sore, bleeding mouth.

*Wednesday Night*

"JUST SQUIRRELS, SEBASTIAN." Aimée pulled herself up from the wet ground, brushed herself off. A run in her stocking, now a mud-coated sleeve, grass clinging to her mascara. Picture-perfect.

In Sebastian's flashlight beam, a quartet of arched squirrel tails disappeared up the linden tree trunk. "Quit scaring the marrow from my bones."

She heard strains of baroque music drift from Agustino's atelier. "Ready?"

Not waiting for his answer, she knocked on the glass door.

A split second passed before Agustino opened the door.

"You stood me up, Agustino—"

He clapped his thick paint-spattered hand over her mouth. Shoved her outside, down the path.

"Go away. Now." His words didn't hide the fear vibrating in his voice. "Forget what I said. Leave."

Had the terrorists coerced him?

"Not until you tell me who murdered Xavierre. How you knew the referendum—"

The tiny camera was powered by a nine-volt battery and could run for up to fifteen hours. Enough for what she needed, she hoped.

She scanned the limestone buildings, the high stone wall opposite, for a location in which to install the camera. Rue Copernic was a one-way street. For a moment, sheltered from the night wind by the wall and buildings, streetlight filtering over the crosshatched metal tree grille, she heard a faint rushing of water.

Opposite, the EAU DE PARIS sign on the wall indicated the reservoir, the one the café waiter had mentioned. The wall must support the aboveground pools. No need for a *sorcière* with a witch-hazel branch to locate water here.

No time to memorize the street and building locations. On the back of her checkbook she sketched the street and the car's location, using the wide, dark green door of the Eau de Paris as a landmark. Given the camera's short range and the darkness, it was impossible to view the whole street, but the microphone would catch the sound of approaching footsteps and guide her.

So she'd attach the camera to the car. If it pulled away, the camera would film the route. She ran her fingers along the rooftop, felt the sunroof lip curve, a space. For now it would work.

She pulled a stick of cassis-flavored gum from the bottom of her bag, chewed it, then attached the gum to the sunroof lip and positioned the camera over it. She activated the camera, clicked the transmitter ON, then checked the receiver.

A woman pushing a stroller emerged from the apartment door behind her. She pulled a blanket over the infant inside and smiled at Aimée. Aimée smiled back, took a few steps, and lifted the receiver to her ear as if talking on her cell phone. The woman stopped a few steps away, putting the brakes on the stroller to converse with a man emerging from an apartment.

A watcher? Lookouts? Surveilling the car?

Aimée hit MUTE on her cell phone, just in case, nodding and pretending to listen to the receiver crooked between her neck and shoulder.

By the time she'd walked halfway down the street, she'd slid the receiver into her coat pocket. With this wireless model, she'd have the car in sight if it kept within fifteen kilometers of her. More than she needed. Unless, with the stash of stolen blank documents and the princess, they left Paris en route to the border. But she couldn't do anything about that right now.

At the end of the street, she checked the monitor in her pocket. The red light blinked in transmission mode. The dark outlines of the Mercedes roof glinted with raindrops.

But she needed a clean cell phone, to hook up to her laptop and record the feed. She needed René's help.

At Place Victor Hugo, the lit fountain sprayed and the taxi waited. She slid into the back seat. "Rue de la Reynie, *s'il vous plaît*." She passed a twenty-franc bill over the leather backrest.

"Eh, you pay at the end," he said, tired eyes under his brown-gray grizzled hair.

"My battery's dead. Mind if use your cell phone? Local call."

"Then I'd have to give you change and. . . ."

"Keep it."

She used the taxi driver's phone and punched in René's number.

"*Oui?*" said René.

"It's Aimée. Has anyone asked about me? Called?"

René cleared his throat. "*Oui*, Madame. Matter of fact, even more than that."

She heard conversations in the background. She shivered. "The EPIGN's at the office, aren't they? Big man, bland face."

"I'd say so," he said.

"Then you haven't heard from me. You're going home, it's late, closing the office," she said. "Bring me a fresh cell phone, too. Leave. Matter of fact, why are you there?"

"Some people need to work, Madame. To pay bills."

As if she didn't?

"I'll meet you in your garage. Ten minutes."

Within ten minutes, the taxi crawled up narrow medieval streets leading to Beaubourg. The soot-stained spires of Saint-Merri loomed, highlighted against the space-age red-and-blue–tubed Centre Pompidou behind it. Her hands shook.

The taxi pulled over under a streetlight. "Monsieur, I'd like to book another hour. Can you wait here?"

*"Pas de problème."*

She kept to the walls on narrow rue Quincampoix, entering the back door of René's garage. The automatic garage door opened and René's DS Citroën rolled in. She waited behind the dustbins until the aluminum shuttered door rolled back down.

Darkness.

Then she felt a gun in her ribs.

*Wednesday Night*

OUT OF BREATH and shaking, Maria scraped a twisted wire into the crumbling concrete surrounding the iron rung holding her leg chain. At this rate, it would take hours to dislodge the rusted iron. Hours she didn't have. She prayed that her father was cooperating with their demands. But for the life of her, she didn't know if he would—after last time. Or if he could.

Only the steady drip of water accompanied Joxi's moans. His tossing and turning raised the goose bumps on her arms. The man was in pain, his condition worsening. And the others had left.

They were alone. Her stomach gnawed with hunger. No food.

His moaning escalated.

Unnerved, she set down the wire, held the chain, and crept over to him. Joxi was covered by a rough blanket, and his sweat-beaded face was flushed. Broken red blood vessels marked a path from his swollen eye; the blood-soaked bandaging crisscrossed his inflamed cheek. Sour smells of sweat emanated from him.

His vise-like grip encircled her wrist. "Ur . . . ur."

A moan, or the Basque word for water? In a stone niche, she saw bottled water among the strewn contents of her bag. She scrabbled her fingers through the objects. No cell phone. Her agenda containing addresses, phone numbers was gone. Fodder for ransom demands?

But she couldn't stand Joxi's moans. Or understand how they'd leave their wounded comrade. Or her. Hadn't the *mec* promised. . . .

Or maybe she didn't want to understand. Didn't want to face the fact that they'd left them to die.

With trembling hands she raised the plastic bottle to Joxi's lips. He gulped, dribbles running down his chin, over the blanket. Again and again, greedy for more.

A small sample-like packet labeled PENICILLIN sat in the stone niche. "How about your medication?"

His dark eyes rolled back in his head. His body arched, then bucked in sharp convulsions. But his grip held like iron. Good god, what could she do?

Was he dying? Having seizures? The fever burned from him like fire.

She lifted his head, opened his mouth, put the antibiotic tablet on his tongue. Closed his mouth. "Chew." Then she emptied the water bottle over his face. Patted his brow, his face, his arms with the now-sopping blanket, trying to cool him down. Phrases in Basque tumbled from his dry lips. Rhythmic, chanting. A Basse Navarre dialect she didn't understand except for occasional Spanish words: tree, boulder, rushing water. What sounded like a child's song.

He lay there, shaking and helpless. White scars ribbed his shoulders, his chest, like welts from an old beating. What kind of life had he lived? she wondered. She'd never nursed her boyfriend like this, or taken care of him. He hated her being nearby if he was sick.

Twenty, thirty minutes passed; she couldn't tell time down here in the dark. She kept on swabbing Joxi down. Finding more bottled water, wetting the blankets until his convulsions subsided into infrequent jerks.

"Hotz . . . no."

Now chills wracked him. His teeth shattered. He grew aware, his eyes darted. For a man of machismo, he acted as helpless as an infant. She didn't know which was worse: his shaking from chills, or convulsing with fever.

How could she find something dry to wrap him in? Why was she doing this when her life depended on getting away?

She found another jacket, a pair of discarded overalls, a stained plastic tarp, and wrapped him as tightly as she could to generate body heat. In the corner she eyed tubes of paper, unrolled them, and covered him like the homeless she'd seen in the doorways covered with newspapers to keep warm. She kept rubbing his arms, his legs, until her shoulders ached. After a while, his shaking subsided; his eyes closed.

She sighed in relief. And realized for the first time that the fear had left her: she'd been too busy. Tired, she leaned down on the earth floor, clasped her arms around her knees to ease her aching back and shoulders.

The kerosene lamp sputtered low on the flickering wick, casting long shadows on the stone. She looked up. Joxi's heavy-lidded, half-open eyes watched her.

"Why?"

She stretched her neck, felt his forehead. "Your fever's down."

"You tied me like a hog for butchering." His one dark eye glittered.

"Against the chills." She tucked the plastic tighter around him. "You were delirious."

His hand shot out, grabbed her hair. Tight. Pulling the roots of her hair. Pain seared her scalp. "Why did you use these?"

"I . . . I took anything to keep you warm." Tears brimmed in her eyes. "You were convulsing with fever, then shaking with cold. That's the thanks I get for. . . ." And then it all hit her: the tiredness, the hunger, being chained up. She burst into sobs.

The look in his eye changed.

"*Miatzte ama,* just like my mother. Shut up." He struggled to sit up. "Roll these up. Put them back as you found them."

She rubbed her head. The chain around her ankle bit and rubbed her skin raw.

"Now," he barked.

She put them together. Diagrams of what looked like train tracks, rail lines. She rolled them back up, slipped them in the tube.

His gaze wavered.

"Why did you help me?"

She blinked. "I don't know. You're a human being?" She shrugged. "Maybe that's stupid. Maybe you're going to kill me."

"That's the plan."

She backed up in fear, shaking her head.

"Will you do two things?" He leaned on his elbow, coughing. "Do them the way I say."

"So I'll die sooner?" She spit on the floor. "Forget it."

He grabbed the lip balm and tweezers from her things. "Slather this in the lock on your ankle chain; twist your tweezers inside until it clicks open."

"Quit playing with me."

"It's gotten me out of jail every time." He looked at his watch on the stone niche. "Now. Do it before they return."

"You don't get it, do you? Your comrades left us to die."

"Comrades? You think a true Basque patriot lines his pockets? Kills an old comrade?" He winced in pain. "I heard the snakes. They thought I'd gone unconscious." He shook his head. "Don't let on. The trick's to act the same. When they load up, make a break."

Surprised, she stared at him.

"How can I get out?"

"You're on your own there." He coughed, a wheezing from deep in his chest. "Now hand me that bag." He pointed to a khaki canvas shoulder bag in the corner.

"Why should I trust you?"

"A life for a life, *compris?*"

"You're making a deal?"

"You're not from the Motherland, eh? Basques always make deals."

Could she trust him? But from the shaking of his hands, the tiny beads of sweat forming again on his brow, she'd gotten the better deal.

*Wednesday Night*

A LIGHTNING CHOP batted Aimée's arm down. The stinging crosscut to her ribs whipped her against the garage wall. She yelled and toppled into the dustbins. Pain seared her side. Choking for breath, she raised her arm to ward off the next blow.

"Now the other arm. So I can see it."

She heard the flick of a switch, and light flooded the underground stone-walled garage.

René stood, legs spread, arms extended in firing stance with a Beretta aimed at her head.

"Nice, René." She gasped. "Register your arms as lethal weapons. Forget the Beretta."

René's grip wavered. "*Mon Dieu,* with the outfit I thought a man—"

"If you bought it, the EPIGN will. That's what counts."

René pocketed the gun, reached down to help her up. "*Désolé,* Aimée. Are you all right? Does it hurt?"

Only when she breathed. She got to her feet. Staggered.

"Let me wrap your ribs. Come upstairs. . . ."

"No time." She pulled out the video receiver, grabbed the

wall as her vision reeled and then righted itself. "I need you to hook this up to your laptop, record and monitor the feed."

René stared at the dim video playing on the palm-sized screen. "But that's the Mercedes. I recognize the roof line."

"That's right, René, parked with stolen plates on rue Copernic." She winced at every breath. "Did you bring me a phone?"

His brow crinkled in worry. He took his cane from the car. "What the hell's going on?"

"I didn't want you involved," she said. "Look, just trust me—"

"Not until you tell me what all this means, why the EPIGN was asking questions."

"There's not much time."

"I'm waiting, Aimée."

So she gave him the short version.

"Kidnapped?" René rocked on his handmade Lobb shoes. "If Euskadi Action, this ETA group, kidnapped the princess using the Mercedes, are they likely to use it again?"

"The stolen plates." She wished she had one of the painkillers sitting on her bedside table.

"They'll abandon it if they're smart," he said.

"Got any other ideas, René?"

He brushed cobwebs from her coat. "I might. Let's go upstairs."

"What if the EPIGN are watching your place?"

René swallowed. "Good point. But Michou's expecting me next door for a drink."

The blood sample from her Louboutins. She still hadn't heard back from Viard.

"If Viard's there, can you ask him to meet us down here?"

René shook his head but punched in the number and made the call. "What about hooking up the feed? Please, René."

In the back seat of the Citroën, René opened his briefcase, set his laptop on the leather seat, and hooked a cable to the receiver.

Not two minutes later, footsteps sounded on her left.

"Giving Michou a run for her money?" Viard grinned. "I like your androgynous look. Very Helmut Newton. But why the cloak and dagger, Aimée?" Viard dusted his hands in the less-than-clean subterranean garage René rented for half the price of his apartment and felt lucky to have.

"You don't want to know, Viard."

"Again?" He pulled a notebook from the breast pocket of his tweed jacket. "We were swamped. I managed to get to your heels this morning. O-negative blood type. Nothing special. Except for the mucosa traces."

"Mucosa?"

"You know, the lining in the nose. After lunch, we had a lull," Viard said. "Thought I'd put a portion of the sample under the microscope. Interesting."

Anxious and hot in the humid dank garage air, she took off the fedora. Shook her hair. "In what way?"

"The mucosa came from the nose. Along with the blood. I'd say there was a nosebleed."

Surprised, she moved closer. "Not from a gunshot wound?"

"I found no gunpowder residue. Of course, that might not present in such a small sample. But, why someone might have a nosebleed: I looked more closely at the blood—red cells, white cells, platelets. . . ." Viard, enthusiasm creeping into his voice, thumbed to another page in his notebook. Nodded as he read and rubbed his chin. "Then it got fascinating, or morbid, depending on your point of view."

Why couldn't he just tell her?

"What's your take, Viard?"

"Far too many white blood cells—abnormal ones at that—for a healthy individual. Also not a normal number of platelets."

"Meaning?"

"I'm not a doctor, Aimée," he said.

"Neither am I, remember?" Her ribs ached. She wished he'd get to the point. "I got through a year of premed and never hit the lab. Chemistry and biology did me in."

"Speaking based on the lab smear, with such a high white blood cell count, he's about done in."

She unsnapped the tie. Fanned her neck. "How can you tell?"

"Like I say, I'm not a physician. But symptoms such as nosebleeds, fatigue, weight loss, and high white blood cell count—and abnormal white blood cells—in most cases indicate an advanced stage of disease. Leukemia."

Stunned, she leaned against the wall. Did she need to rethink everything with this revelation?

"A terminal terrorist? Gives him an interesting motive," René said.

"Worse, René," she said, thinking. "Nothing to lose."

She pecked Viard on both cheeks. *"Merci."*

"So when's our dinner?"

"Ask René," she said. "I've got to go."

"But it's safer here," he said. "Stay with Michou."

"My taxi meter's running."

René handed her a red cell phone. "That's your new number. It's programmed in my cell. Keep in touch every twenty minutes."

She paused at the door, a dark unease flooding her. Morbier's weight loss, the hollows under his eyes. "How long does the man have, Viard?"

"I run the lab, but I don't provide diagnoses, Aimée," he said.

"But according to . . . the platelets, your observations. . . ." Her throat caught.

"At this point, I'd suggest he live every day like it's his only one."

*　*　*

AIMÉE SURVEILLED THE winding street, the corners. Deserted except for the taxi. She clutched her side, sinking into the back seat. "Rue Raynouard, s'il vous plaît. On the way, stop at the all-night pharmacy on Champs-Elysées."

Ten minutes and three extra-strength Dolipranes—washed down by fizzy Vittel—later, she crouched in the back seat as the taxi cruised past Xavierre's dark, shuttered town house. She noted the parked cars and the Renault with two heads silhouetted against the darkness. The Renault from the market.

Across the narrow street, she noted a dim glow emanating through Madame de Boucher's second-floor lace curtains. Then a darker curtain blocked the dim light.

A car door slammed, an engine rumbled, and the Renault's headlights flashed on.

"Turn right." Past the steepled church on rue Jean Bologne, paralleling rue Raynouard, she motioned for him to pause. "Wait by the florist's across from the Boulainvilliers Métro." She took his card. "If I don't call you within one hour, erase my record. Put me down as a no-show pickup. You never heard of me."

She passed him two hundred francs.

"Deal?"

He nodded, took the francs, patted a tattered copy of a Simenon novel on his dashboard. "Got an Inspector Maigret investigation to keep me company. Almost as exciting as tonight."

She summoned a smile. "But tonight's far from over, Monsieur."

She knew Madame de Boucher's building on rue Alphonse XIII overlooked the rear courtyards and gardens of these apartments.

Stepping onto the narrow street, she had a sense of being watched. She heard the crunching of leaves, the heavy tread of measured footsteps.

Her shoulders tightened. She stepped into the building doorway and turned.

Headlights backlit a dark figure: moisture glimmering on close-cropped hair, a martial stride halfway down the street. Hair rose on the back of her neck. No mistaking that cocky assuredness. EPIGN.

They not only were watching Xavierre's house, they were patrolling the *quartier.*

She dug in her purse for the stubby universal mailman's key in the side pocket. The one she'd "borrowed" from Morbier a month ago and "forgotten" to return. The worn key provided *la Poste* universal access to buildings and courtyards. A *passe-partout.* Where was it?

The footsteps crackling over the leaves got closer. She concentrated until her fingers found the key.

Praying that the key still worked, she inserted it and heard the lock tumble. Once inside, she shut the glass door, heading into the marble-tiled foyer toward the rear. She kept going, ignoring the knocking coming from the glass door, almost running into the table with a vase of roses emitting a faint fragrance.

At the door on her right, she slipped off her boots and stuck them in her bag. *Sans* stilettos, she crept across the dark pavered inner courtyard to what had been a carriage entrance. Now a small wooden vaulted door was the only egress.

The door creaked open onto the adjoining courtyard, choked with Land Rovers, a barometer of the *quartier's* wealth. A high stone wall backed onto Madame's building.

No trees to climb. No outbuilding with a roof. No ladder.

Stuck.

Less than two hours left.

She climbed onto the nearest Land Rover's hood and then to its roof, eyeballed a rough measurement, and wished the Doliprane would dull the ache in her ribs faster. She fashioned a slipknot at one end of her cashmere scarf, knotting the other end to her long, coarser wool scarf. Together they almost reached the top of the wall.

And then she saw the wood wine carton filled with newspapers. Climbing down, she spread old newspapers on the Land Rover's roof, hefted the cartons, and prayed her aim would hit the rusted iron remains of the old gas-lamp fixture topping the wall.

She balanced on the upside-down wine carton and threw the end of her scarf. Missed. Then again. On her third try, the scarf knot caught on the rusted iron and held. She tugged, testing her weight, and climbed, pulling herself up.

Her toes wedged in the stone niches. She tried to ignore the sharp slicing pain as her sore ribs landed on the wall's top ledge. Then she levied herself up. One leg over, and the next. She gasped in pain.

Below her lay a huge drop to Madame's courtyard.

She prayed to god her scarves would hold and rappelled halfway down the wall before the rotted iron in the crumbling stone came loose. She caught the ivy trellis and hung suspended,

the pain in her side shooting through her, then eased herself
down onto a chipped haloed statue of Mary.

Perspiring, she picked up her knotted scarves, now encrusted
with rust. Keep going, she told herself. She had to keep going.

She crept past the concierge's loge and jiggled the inner door
lock with the mini-screwdriver on her Swiss Army knife until it
clicked open. She slipped on her boots and mounted the staircase to Madame de Boucher's door.

The strains of "Leaves of Autumn" came from the doorway.
That damn bird was singing again. She knocked and stuck her
fedora over the peephole. Heard footsteps on the other side. She
knocked again.

"Madame, please, I must talk with you."

No answer.

"It's vital, Madame. The *quartier*'s thick with police patrols."

"So," came a muffled voice. "You're with the police. I know
the law. Go away. You can't barge in here until dawn. Nazis or
not, you won't get in here."

Aimée took out her card and slipped it under the door. "I lied.
I'm not a *flic*. Look at my card. Irati's in danger. Please, I'm the
only one who can help her."

Silence. She removed the fedora and put her eye to the peephole.

"Agustino was murdered not far from here. Tell Irati. But he
warned me before her mother's murderer. . . ."

The door opened. Madame de Boucher stood, ice pick raised.
"Shhh . . . my neighbors. Quick."

Again in that hallway reeking of old newspapers. But a
quivering Irati, her face drained pale, stood by the coatrack.

"But how did you know I'd . . . ?"

"Come here? A good guess. You Socialists stick together,

don't you?" Aimée stepped inside. "Listen, the EPIGN's parked below, watching your house. They're looking for me too." The parrot's singing was louder inside. The shrill notes grated on her taut nerves, and she shut the salon door. "It's dangerous; I know a safe hiding place."

"You're lying." Irati backed up.

"Check for yourself," she said.

Madame de Boucher set down the ice pick and grabbed her walking stick. "I'll see about that."

"This man coerced you, didn't he, Irati?"

Irati backed away. Her eyelids fluttered. "I don't know what you mean."

Of course she did. Just her body movement gave her away.

"Do you want him to get away with your mother's murder? The brutal slaying of Agustino and his nephew . . . ?" She shuddered, remembering the bloodied Adidas. Blood everywhere.

Panic painted Irati's tight features.

"Agustino told me he's called Txili, his ETA *nom de guerre*," Aimée said. "What hold did he have over your mother?"

Irati bit her lip. "*Maman* told me nothing. I saw him, this Txili, yes; but *Maman* told me to get out of the room. I'd never seen him in my life. I didn't know he'd stolen our car or what he wanted until the next morning." A pinprick of blood showed on her chapped lip.

Aimée nodded. "But was he bleeding? Did he look wounded? Could you tell that much?"

She thought, shrugged. "He coughed, I think." Irati's brow wrinkled in worry. "On the phone, he said *Maman* had left the bag for him; I was to do as she'd promised or he couldn't protect us."

"Couldn't protect you from what?"

"The others. The group. That's what he kept saying." Her lip trembled. "They'd place a bomb under Robbé's car, shove me on the Métro tracks, my aunt would return to Bayonne and find my uncle dead. Terrible things. He said he couldn't stop them unless I cooperated."

"And you believed him?"

Irati's eyes batted in fear. "What else could I do?"

"But you're involved with Euskadi Action. This shows all their trademarks."

"Involved?" Irati spread her arms. "I attended one meeting. I wish I never had. Fanatics ranting about reclaiming the Basque homeland, like a religion. They insisted I buy a stupid T-shirt and hound me now with mail."

So that's how they'd gotten her address.

"But what did this Txili hold over your mother?"

"*Zut alors,* we can't get away from them. Anywhere Robbé goes, his car could go up in smoke. If I'm in a crowded station. . . ." She shook her head. "Any time, he said, any place, it could happen."

He'd terrorized her. Irati saw his threats as real. Who was to say they weren't? But how could she break through and convince her?

"I can help you," Aimée said. "Or there's the EPIGN downstairs. The elite assault squad. It's just a matter of time until they find you, like I did. They'll interrogate you, break you down, link you to the princess's kidnapping."

Irati's hand went to her mouth in fear. "The princess . . . what do you mean?"

"I think you know. At least part of it."

She hoped her hunch was right.

Tears brimmed Irati's eyes. "But I never knew. Never. He just told me. . . ." Her shoulders shook. "You think he'll hurt Maria?"

"Not if I can help it," she said, pulling a cane-backed chair toward her. "Sit down. We've got less than two hours left."

"Two hours?"

"His deadline. Have a seat."

Irati collapsed in the chair. "Her father was ambassador here years ago. That's how we knew them. Maria's family comes to Bayonne every summer. We go to my uncle's house in the mountains in Basse Navarre. I've known Maria since we were little. She likes to party, a little rebellious. But still, inside, she's *sympa*, you know; she has a good heart."

"Spoiled brat, I heard."

Irati wiped her eyes. "Her father's so conservative, insists she perform her 'duties' *noblesse oblige*. She hates it. A little wild, yes. But I figured she'd go along with it."

"With a kidnapping by ETA terrorists, a daring escape, followed by a tell-all article and modeling contract?"

"Nothing like that." Irati shook in horror. "He insisted that I ask Maria to meet at this resto and say we'd go clubbing and then . . ." She paused. "It felt wrong. He said *Maman* was a patriot and wasn't I? When I asked him what he meant, he said *Maman* owed the cause from way back. Took an oath. Had vowed support."

"Support that got her killed? How could he explain her murder?"

"At first he blamed Morbier." She rubbed her eyes. "Then he changed his story, said he couldn't control the *ettaras*—the young militants—who took things into their own hands out in the garden."

"A lie," Aimée said. "Like all the lies he's telling you. I only heard one person's footsteps, one car door slam." Aimée took Irati's elbow, stared into her tear-filled eyes. "He's using your fear, I understand. But you can't let Morbier go down for this."

"But he threatened that Robbé would be next if I didn't cooperate, didn't arrange to meet Maria."

"So instead of the Marmottan reception announcing the Basque accord, Maria went to meet you but was kidnapped instead."

"You're sure?" Irati's eyes batted in fear. "I've heard nothing on the radio or *télé*."

"I was there. Before any public announcement was made, her father insisted on a three-hour window, to negotiate in private."

"I don't understand."

"The Basque referendum's dead in the water and Maria's the hostage for release of ETA's political prisoners in France, his goal all along."

Irati blinked. "He's an ETA political militant? You're sure? He seems a business type, conservative. I couldn't believe the way he talked."

Aimée's mind spun into high gear. "As if his talk doesn't match his appearance?"

"I saw him for only a few minutes before *Maman* . . ." Irati took a breath. ". . . made me leave. At first impression I took him for a banker. Thinking back, yes. Now in his phone calls he uses those old phrases, *passé* ETA slogans, 'militant patriotism' and 'Basque autonomy.' People don't talk like that any more. They're sick of violence."

A front? But for what?

Irati stared at her. "He said he knows you."

The hair stood on the back of her neck. "Me?"

"He must have seen you, I don't know."

Of course: from the window. Or . . . something in the back of her mind niggled, eluding her.

"But at first you didn't recognize me in this outfit, did you,

Irati? That's why you're going to get away—you can change clothes like shedding skin, new colors, new hair."

"But for how long?"

Irati had no illusions about the future, but a desperate need to believe. How many more bodies would there be, she wondered, before Irati wised up?

"Long enough for you to—"

The cell phone on the hall radiator trilled. Irati glanced at the number. "It's him." Before she could answer, Aimée grabbed her hand.

"Keep him talking as long as you can," she said. "Agree to anything. Ask to meet him. Just keep him on the line."

Irati nodded and picked up the telephone, her eyes wide with fear.

"*Oui?*"

Pause. "Look, there's something. . . ."

She pursed her lips.

"What . . . *non!*"

Irati dropped the phone.

Aimée reached down and grabbed it. A buzz. She hit CALL-BACK and the number came up blocked. Not even time for Léo to trace it.

Irati looked like she'd been hit by a truck.

"He's got Robbé."

Aimée's heart sank. She was in over her head. All their heads. For a moment she weighed working with Valois and informing the EPIGN, people she didn't trust farther than her little finger.

But doing that would link Irati to ETA, the kidnapping, Agustino's murder, the stolen documents. A barbed-wire tangle of complications. And might get her no further toward finding the murderer or the princess.

"What does he want?"

"He called Robbé 'insurance.'" Irati folded her arms over her chest, rocked. "You see, he told me if talked to anyone, or someone followed me. . . ."

"So you'd get further implicated?" She held the shiny blue virgin passport. "ETA *ettaras* robbed the *Imprimerie Nationale* van, killed a *flic*. They kept their stash at Agustino's. I found this in his atelier."

"I don't know. That's all he said. I heard Robbé shouting. A scream."

She covered her face with shaking hands.

Aimée's new phone trilled. She went into the salon to take the call. The bird, quiet for the moment, pecked at the cuttle bone in the cage.

"See anything, René?"

"I hear something on rue Copernic," he said. "The car door's opening."

Her heart jumped.

"Dim image, distorted pixels," said René. "All sepia, dark. The streetlight's far away. Talking. No response. I think it's a cell phone conversation. But the viewfinder's out of range, just catches dark movement . . . wait, like an arm reaching into the car."

"Can you make out words?"

All of a sudden the bird burst into a shrill "Leaves of Autumn" refrain.

"Wait, I heard the same voice two minutes earlier on the street. I'm recording so I can clean up the audio . . . now a damn truck. . . ."

"But he's in the car? Driving away?"

"*Non.* A head, but I can't make it out. . . . Who's singing in the background?"

"A damn parrot," she said. "Call me back."

Frustrated, she wanted to kick the bird's cage and ruffle more than his feathers. Instead, she covered his cage with the cloth; silence reigned, apart from Irati's muffled sobbing.

"Irati, tell him the truth," she said. "You're being watched, trailed. Would he want you to lead them right to him? What does he want from you?"

Irati averted her eyes. She was keeping something back.

"Do you want Robbé alive?"

She nodded. "I don't have any other choice but to do what he says."

"We all have choices. Just not necessarily the ones we want."

"Easy for you to say."

"The EPIGN want me to work for them. I can easily lean out the window and say, 'Up here.' Should I? They're a trained elite assault unit that tallies the enemy body count as success and victims as collateral damage. Otherwise, by yourself, you're depending on this man who killed your mother and Agustino."

"How do you know he killed *Maman*? Why?"

"I know Morbier didn't. He was meeting an informer on the Paris outskirts." She expelled air from her mouth. "Cooperating with Txili gives neither Robbé nor the princess a shot in hell of living more than an hour and a half."

Aimée took the encryption manual from her bag, thumbed to the blank back page.

"So, three choices: the big boys with big toys, or you on your own playing to Txili's drum, or me," she said. "Me, I guarantee you'll have a shot. Maybe just one, but that's more than zero. So you choose, Irati."

"You think they're dead no matter what, don't you?"

"Going by the statistics so far, a wise assumption."

Irati's face crinkled in pain.

"What's the point now? He'll get to us. I know it. Robbé's diabetic. His insulin—"

"Do you have it?" Aimée interrupted.

Irati's head bobbed. "I always carry extra for him, in case."

Aimée pushed the damp hair from Irati's tear-stained face.

"Then we have to get it to him, *n'est-ce pas?*" she said. "It's a good bargaining tool. I have an idea. Do you want to hear it?"

Irati wiped her face with her sleeve, nodded.

Aimée took her pencil and started writing.

"First you'll tell him this," she said, "but in your own words."

Irati stared at Aimée's encryption manual. Nodded again.

Now she had her.

"After that, you'll tell me about Robbé."

\* \* \*

MADAME DE BOUCHER made a tsk-tsk sound. "I saw the scum. Time for you to escape."

Madame stood at the hall armoire, one hand on her ebony walking stick, her other selecting a coat for Irati. She took a seventies belted checked-wool coat—never worn, by the look of it. Sniffed. "A little mothball odor. Not bad." She handed it to Irati with an Hermès scarf.

"This way," Madame de Boucher said. "We used it during the war."

Hadn't been used since, Aimée figured from the rotting timbers, speckled mold, and dirt-filmed broken glass in the back stairs. Madame opened a cobwebbed cupboard, tapped her walking-stick tip inside. Creaking and groaning, the cupboard moved to reveal a blacked-over skylight. "I keep it oiled. *Les Fritz* never found this. Good thing, eh, you never know."

Oiled for more than fifty years. Amazing.

"Too bad it didn't save my brother. Aaah, but that's another story."

Aimée twisted the handle and pushed. The slanted skylight gave a centimeter. "Harder," Madame said.

Using her knee, she wedged it open enough to squeeze through. Cold night air and pigeon feathers met her.

"Follow along the roof line to the last building."

"And then?"

"Find the blacked-out skylight, wedge it open with this." Madame handed Irati a hammer, then tied the Hermès scarf around Irati's head. *"Bon courage."*

Aimée'd need more than that, considering the slick blue roof tiles, a multi-story drop, and a shaking Irati.

She handed Irati the end of her tied scarves. "Hold on. Don't look down. No matter what."

Algae-scented wind from the Seine gusted over her skin, making her lapels fly up. Beyond lay a vista of glittering pinprick lights as she crawled, edging along the narrow rooftop. Caked pigeon droppings, crackling twig birds' nests, and crumbling brick came back on her fingers. She took deep breaths, cold air slicing into her lungs, her gaze focused on the next rooftop. Then the next, inching her way forward along the narrow ridge.

Skittering stucco clumps slid down the roof tiles. She had to keep breathing, keep going, aiming for the dark misted outline of the last roof. Trying to imagine a young Madame de Boucher doing this.

"Almost there, Irati."

"Get going now," the girl yelled. She pushed him up the stairs.

Few stars shone above them in the night sky. A half-moon wisped by clouds hung over the Arc de Triomphe, a postage stamp–sized yellow glow in the distance. Faint lights glimmered on the surface of swimming pool–like reservoirs. She inhaled the algae-scented wind, heard the splash of a fish. To the right, the blue-lit needle of the Eiffel Tower poked behind the building rooftops. From below, one would never know that several stories above the street, a whole other world existed.

"That way. Quick." She pointed toward the far end of the smallest pool, calculating the direction of rue Paul Valéry. They had to escape. A long narrow walkway rimmed the pool at the rear of the dark stone walls of apartment buildings.

Running now, she made out the nineteenth-century two-story mansard-roofed house, quaint and incongruous, at the edge of the water. Unlived-in, dark, with torn shades in the window. It reminded her of a village train station complete with geraniums, similar to the gatehouse at the rue Copernic entrance.

The exit. She had to find the exit to the street. In the crusted brick wall edging the house, she saw another green metal door.

"Hurry. Go to the door."

The girl ran, coat flapping in the wind, Robbé behind, trying to keep up. She took the key ring, tried the larger old-fashioned keys first. None fit.

"I don't like this," the girl said, her voice quavering. "Hear that?"

Shouts carried over the water.

The girl balled her wool sleeve around her fist and punched in the glass panel of the house's door. Glass splintered, caught the light, and sprayed the coat like shiny sequins. She reached in and turned the old-fashioned handle. "Locked," she gasped. "What do we do?"

Aimée's mind raced. Should they try to break down the door, barricade themselves inside, and call for help? Who knew how long she could hold them off?

But she couldn't give up. Finally, the last key clicked and turned. "Let's go."

Running down the narrow, dark stairs between the reservoir foundations and brick walls, she hit the taxi driver's number on her cell phone.

"*Vite!* Rue Paul Valéry, near the corner of rue Lauriston."

If a reception committee was waiting, she hoped the taxi would deter them.

She turned the key in the last door to the street.

"Whatever happens, turn right and get into the G7 taxi."

The girl rubbed her runny nose with her sleeve, nodding.

"Can you do that, Robbé?"

"What about you?" he said sullenly.

She pulled the gun out of the girl's coat pocket. "Just don't look back, okay?"

"Look, I'm sorry I. . . ."

"Forget it. Go."

She stepped out, the gun raised. Four dark figures were in the middle of rue Paul Valéry, the taxi idling at the corner behind them.

She hit the taxi driver's cell number again. "See those *mecs*? I'm sure you can scare them. There's three of us just beyond them. Whatever you do, don't let them reach us."

A little laugh. "*Pas de problème.*"

All of a sudden, the taxi gunned down the street, headlights blinking, horn blaring. The *mecs* jumped and scattered. With a squeal of brakes, the taxi stopped in front of Aimée.

She opened the door and pushed the others into the back seat, then climbed in front beside the driver.

Without a word, he ground into first, tore down rue Paul Valéry and into Avenue Victor Hugo. In a few blocks, he pulled into the roundabout of Place de l'Étoile circling the Arc de Triomphe, a maze of headlights and hundreds of darting cars. He opened his window, stuck his fist out at a driver who slowed, then cut in front of a truck. He grinned at Aimée, his eyes shining. "No one can follow us here. We'll be lucky to get out alive ourselves."

"Great job," she said.

"I haven't had this much fun in years," he said.

"*Bon*, let's keep circling and I'll make some calls, figure out where we're going next."

She turned to the girl in the back seat. "We haven't been introduced. I'm Aimée, and you are . . . ?"

"Maria."

"I thought so," she said. "Your father's looking for you."

Robbé sat back, rubbing his arm. "That's an understatement."

\* \* \*

AFTER CIRCLING THE Arc de Triomphe for twenty minutes, the taxi turned into Avenue Foch, the wide, tree-lined boulevard radiating from Place de l'Étoile. Town house after fashionable town house and mansion after mansion lined the street. The taxi pulled up to a grilled metal gate. A security guard nodded to the taxi driver. The automatic gates opened to a driveway where there was an ambulance standing. The ambassador paced on the front steps of the town house, which had lights blazing in every window.

Aimée turned to Maria. "Remember what we said? Forget my using the gun. But describe the Basque who helped you, the rail-line diagrams, and everything else you remember."

Maria swallowed. "The ambassador doesn't look too happy. I think I'm in big trouble."

"Wrong. You're giving him a feather in his diplomatic hat. You're safe, Maria. Don't let him forget it."

Maria gave a small smile and struggled out of the coat. "Wouldn't want to forget this." Her torn chemise hung from her thin bruised shoulders.

Aimée pressed a card with Martine's number into her hand. "Call my friend Martine, the journalist, in a little while. You can trust her."

A grim-faced ambassador, in rolled-up shirtsleeves, his tie loosened, opened the taxi door. Without a word, he took Maria's arm, helped her up the steps, and gestured to the waiting paramedics.

He'd left a calling card on the coat. A military-issue satellite cell phone with built in GPS tracking. Courtesy of Colonel Valois.

Just what she'd feared. Sitting in a taxi on the wealthiest street in Paris didn't equate with fighting rebels in the mountains of Afghanistan.

Or did it?

According to Léo, the moment she flicked on the phone it would activate the GPS, alerting the military, who would immediately track her location. Deal with the devil? She needed to think about that. Figure out how to use it to her advantage.

The phone rang.

Of course, the thing was already on.

Robbé handed it to her.

"Mademoiselle Leduc," said Colonel Valois. "Interesting solo operation. Our team would have handled it with more efficiency and a lower body count."

She doubted that. His formerly inviting tone had turned frosty. Maybe he wanted to take back his offer.

"So you say, Colonel," she said. "I guess you had to be there."

Pause. "If my men told me that, I'd remind them of the families left behind."

Sanctimonious bastard.

"Next time a terrorist's ready to rape a young girl and puts a gun to the head of a man in diabetic shock, I'll try to remember that." She bit her tongue. Stupid to provide fodder for an investigation.

"That's besides the point, Mademoiselle Leduc," he said. "Our mission's not accomplished."

"You've got the princess—"

"I'm referring to loose ends," he interrupted. "I think you know what I mean. It's very much in your interest to cooperate."

So now he'd twist shooting a Basque terrorist in self-defense against her? Big boys with big toys, Martine had said, and frustrated at not using them. Her intuition told her to act interested in working for him.

"So, don't I get paid now?"

"Did I imply that?" His tone warmed. "The offer stands. *Bien sûr*, and according to our terms. Our protocol, that's the way we operate."

He sounded like the IT director client at the failing company, whose "protocol" ultimately couldn't pay Leduc's fees.

"I'm listening."

"Keep this phone operational at all times. The moment you're contacted, respond. Oh, and alert me if you get any calls on the phone in your bag." Pause. "No more solo operations. Just keep me informed and we'll take it from there."

In other words, stay glued to them by GPS, every movement tracked.

"You're interested in hearing my terms, Colonel?"

"We've already set up a bank account with—"

"I didn't finish, Colonel," she said. "Commissaire Morbier released and cleared of all charge. C'*est tout.*"

"But that's not my jurisdiction, Mademoiselle."

She stared at the lighted mansions beyond the trees flashing by.

"I'm sure you can work something out, Colonel."

She flipped the phone closed and hit the OFF button.

She turned to Robbé. "We've got places to go."

Robbé bit his lip. "I want to see Irati."

"Soon," she said. "Let's go, Monsieur. Of course, we never had that passenger, never came here, *compris?*"

The taxi driver put on his driving gloves and shifted into first. "Understood." His eyes glittered. "Any chance of a car chase?"

"I hope not," she said.

He shrugged. As agreed, the grilled metal gate opened and the taxi merged onto Avenue Foch. Ten minutes later, the taxi parked in front of Fondation d'Auteuil, the church-and-orphanage complex off rue de la Fontaine.

She noticed Robbé's whitened knuckles on the insulin kit. "I think you've got things to tell me, *non?*"

"How did you know I live here?"

"Let's talk inside." She nodded to the taxi driver. "Monsieur. . . ."

He took the Maigret novel from the dashboard. "I know. Reading time." He winked. "Wouldn't trade this job for the world. I'm having the night of my life! And call me Théo."

"Merci, Théo," she said. "But it's not over yet."

Robbé pressed the numbers on the digicode pad with shaking fingers. The gate opened to a long park. The secondhand charity shop with donations from the chic parishioners on the left, the faint outlines of L'église Sainte Thérèse ahead. The orphanage's workshops, offices, and housing on the right.

"You grew up here, Robbé," she said, pulling the coat back on and buttoning it against the dank chill.

"What's that got to do with anything?" he said.

A sign pointed the way upstairs to the orphanage's housing, indicating a wing of shared rooms for young working apprentices like Robbé. A community setting in which to dwell while mastering a trade and avoid steep Paris rents. Apprenticeships, like those of the traditional guilds. The communal meeting room, with blue and yellow chintz curtains, was dark.

"The Basques sponsored your apprenticeship in the Bayonne printing works," Aimée said. "That's where you met Txili, didn't you? The others?"

"What?"

"Irati told me about you," she said. "Your life." Now she had to press him. Get him to reveal Txili. "That's why you wanted a small wedding. As an orphan, you had no family to invite."

He looked away. "We wanted an intimate ceremony," he said, his lisp more pronounced.

"But Xavierre got involved. Of course she meant well, her only daughter, so excited, but it got out of hand," Aimée said.

"Then Txili, your old patron, appeared at the wedding rehearsal party, so happy for you. He wanted to help. He just asked a little favor. After all, you're Basque. Wasn't that what he told you? It was why he'd sponsored you, after all. He knew your ETA patriot parents had been killed in a shootout with the French police."

"*Non . . . non*, I don't know what you're talking about."

"But you do, Robbé. That's why he counted on you with the princess."

"You don't know that. You can't prove that," he said, moving away.

"Not yet," she said. "But what happens when Irati discovers the truth? That you murdered her mother?" she said, trying to provoke him. "Of course, you didn't mean for that to happen, nor for Agustino to die; you didn't know—"

"Stop." He put his hands over his ears.

"But you were worried that Xavierre had told Morbier, a *flic*, the real plan. . . ."

"I didn't kill Xavierre," he yelled. "She helped me, believed in me. Why would I? I give you my word."

She believed him, but his wild eyes and jittery hand movements worried her.

"Then who did, Robbé?" she asked.

His shoulders shook. He opened his mouth to speak. Several short *thupts* sounded, thudding into the arch above them, spitting stone dust over her head. His words froze on his lips.

"Down!" She lunged, pushing him onto the ground.

Another *thupt* and more dust. A high-powered pistol with a suppressor. She crawled under the stone wall. Took a breath and peered over the ledge. A figure flashed under the trees. She heard crunching gravel, the clang of the street gate.

Robbé bolted. She heard his footsteps racing up the stairs.

She took off, skirting the trees, and made it through the gate. Jumped into the taxi. "Which way did he go, Théo?"

She heard the radio tuned low to the talk-radio channel. The open book lay in his lap.

"Théo, wake up." She shook his shoulder. His head tilted, fell onto his chest. The streetlight beam revealed the line of blood running from his ear.

She gasped. Horror-stricken, she put her fingers on his neck. No pulse.

Her fault. She'd caused this poor man's murder. Having the night of his life . . . now she knew what Valois meant. Maybe Théo had grandchildren. She'd been an idiot to think she could do this alone.

Her eye caught on the book. The bright red droplets spattered over the pages. Like the blood pattern on the gravel. As if the killer had leaned in the window to talk to Théo and had a nosebleed when he did the job.

And that's how she could find him.

She jumped out of the taxi and stared at the dim pavement. A faint blood spatter on rue de la Fontaine. Then it stopped at the corner. Which way?

She turned up rue Ribera. A narrow uphill street, cobbled and dark, past the Romanian Maronite church. He'd go slower than her because of his condition, his nosebleed; he'd be trying to stanch the blood. She reached the corner of rue de la Source.

Nothing.

A cough. Faint, as if he was trying to smother it going up the hill. And it hit her.

Of course he knew her. They'd met in the Basque resto.

She ran across the intersection, perspiring now. Up a steeper narrow street, lined by solid nineteenth-century façades with ornate scrolled pilasters, cast-iron balconies, and cherub-adorned portals. Ivy rustled to the right of a boarded-up *hôtel particulier* under reconstruction. Creaking wood, then what sounded like footsteps echoing down a passage between the buildings. She paused, sniffed. A trail of cigar smoke wafted in his wake.

She searched the boarded-up entrance. Fingered the wood and found the handle, sliding open the makeshift entry, and stepped inside. She tiptoed past concrete mixers in the damp narrow walkway to the rear that ended at a crumbling stone wall. On the right, a sagging door in a rotted frame led to what had been a kitchen, the windows broken, now filled with leaves.

She pulled out her penlight, her pulse racing, illuminating a high-ceilinged salon with streaking water stains on the peeling wallpaper. The reek of dampness and rot everywhere was punctuated by the acrid whiff of cigar smoke. Down the creaking hallway, her penlight, a small yellow trail, shone on leaves and more leaves.

A sharp wind sliced from the broken windows with metal bars. Sweat beaded her chin; her body shivered hot and cold. For a moment, she wanted to turn back. Listen to the voice in her head yelling go back. But he'd gotten away from her before. Not this time!

She made her feet move.

She emerged into what had been the ballroom, half roofed, half opened up to the cold sky. Crystals tinkled from the remains of a sagging chandelier hanging perilously from the crossbeams. The dank-walled ballroom's tall doors were boarded up, enclosed on all sides, lit only by the pallor of the moon. Crates and old doors were crammed in the shadows. There were holes in the ripped-up floorboards.

One way in. The same way out. Not good.

Why hadn't she kept that hammer?

The pistol in her pocket contained one more bullet. Where was he? Aiming for a distraction, she shoved the crates aside on her left. Heard the splinter of wood as they crashed onto the floor.

With a quick step she darted in the opposite direction.

"Let's talk, since we're old friends, Beñat," she said. "At least that's how you introduced yourself. You were Timo Baptista in your student days, or do you prefer Txili?"

She felt her way along the damp wall. The smell of cigar smoke intensified. He couldn't suppress his coughing. And then she saw his reflection in the cracked, age-spotted, gold-framed mirror propped against the wall.

He shook his head of close-cropped white hair, a sad expression on his face. His expensive coat hung from his shoulders. "I liked you. Chic, edgy, full of *joie de vivre*. What happened?"

As if she'd personally let him down. If she wasn't careful, he'd charm her again, as he had over olives in the Basque bar.

"But you changed," he said, stepping forward. He tossed the burning cigarillo onto the floor. Ground it out with his foot. "You've become a problem."

She leveled the pistol at him, her back pinned against the rotted doors.

The force of his kick knocked the pistol from her hand and spun it to the floor. Before she could reach for it and grab it, he shoved the gun into a hole in the broken floor with his foot. A plunk and splash of water. Now the gun was in the sewers. Stupid. She'd let her guard down. Perspiration dampened her collar; her shirt stuck to her spine.

"But you're full of surprises," Beñat said, his own pistol in his hand now.

"You didn't need to kill Théo."

"The old taxi driver? Not my fault he tried to play the hero."
A shrug.

He sickened her.

"Just an obstacle in your way, so you took care of him?"

"These things happen," he said.

She had to think her way out of this. Stop him any way she
could. But how?

"You're dying, Beñat," she said, a low throb again in her ribs.
"Leukemia. Such a waste. Look at the cost. And for what?"

Shock mingled with irritation on his hollowed-out face.
Aimée noticed his thinness. "A cold? You call a chest cold leukemia?"

"It's eating you up," she said. "The coat's hanging off you, with
all the weight you've lost."

"So now you're a doctor?" He snorted. "Bunch of quacks.
Never listened to one a day in my life."

"But you're tired, *non?* Those nosebleeds, weakness. . . ."

"Weak? I just kicked a gun out of your hands." He gave a short
laugh. "I thought you were smarter, Detective. I researched you.
I know all about you and the dwarf."

"René?" Her hand went to her mouth.

"He drives a classic Citroën. A collector's item, eh? But for
how long?"

René, in danger from the Basque terrorists, a bomb planted in
his car? She flicked open the GPS phone in her pocket, hit the
ON switch. A beep.

"What's that?"

"Research, you say?" She spoke fast to distract him. "Let's talk
about the police lab's research. They've analyzed the blood
samples from my shoe. Your blood."